Angharad

The second tale from Tan Y Bryn

♥♥

by

Mel Alanson

Copyright © 2020. Mel Alanson. All rights reserved.

This story is fictional, as are the characters depicted. Any resemblance to real persons, living or dead, or actual events is coincidental.

Table of Contents

Chapter 1 1
Chapter 2 8
Chapter 3 22
Chapter 4 27
Chapter 5 31
Chapter 6 34
Chapter 7 43
Chapter 8 48
Chapter 9 55
Chapter 10 62
Chapter 11 71
Chapter 12 84
Chapter 13 94
Chapter 14 100
Chapter 15 104
Chapter 16 110
Chapter 17 115
Chapter 18 120
Chapter 19 124
Chapter 20 134
Chapter 21 142
Chapter 22 147
Chapter 23 161
Chapter 24 168
Chapter 25 177
Chapter 26 183
Chapter 27 184
Chapter 28 190
Chapter 29 197
Glossary of terms 201
Summary of Book 1 203

Chapter 1

Steam rose from the hob, carrying a slightly spicy, but deliciously agreeable, aroma. Angharad Lloyd had arrived home a short while before her teenage son, Denny, and she was now in the kitchen preparing the evening meal.

Denny came into the room, whistling. "Hi Mom. That smells great."

"Hello, Son. It's a stir fry – your favourite. You sound cheerful. What have you been up to today?"

"Oh, you know – this and that. I went round to my mate Kevin's. He's got a new motorbike, and he's promised to show me how to ride it."

"Oh yes?" Angharad lifted the wok, tossing the contents with the sort of dexterity normally associated with a skilled chef – rather than an assistant in a grocery store. She considered Denny's statement for a moment, and felt a twinge of unease. "You be careful now, Denny. Don't get involved in anything dodgy. No riding on the road without insurance – or else just ride it off road."

"Don't worry. mom. I won't do anything daft."

Angharad placed a mug of hot coffee on the table for Denny. "I'm not all that keen on motorbikes, but at least if you had a motorbike – or even one of those scooters, it would give you a bit more flexibility work-wise. You wouldn't be limited to looking for work locally. I do wish you could find something permanent that you'd enjoy. There's not a lot of work out there anyway – and I'm not sure you'd cope with working in a shop. It's driving me crackers, and you're even more of an outdoor type than I am."

"I guess a motorbike would be useful. I'm not really looking forward to cycling to and from Tan Y Bryn – especially with all those hills, and all – but with luck, I'll be able to save a bit of money for a motorbike before the winter sets in."

"Tan Y Bryn? I'm afraid you've lost me Denny. Tan Y Bryn? What are you talking about?"

Denny grinned. "Oh, sorry mom, I forgot to tell you. I went down to see Glyn at the farm today, and he offered me a job. Full time, mind you. I start next Monday."

Angharad squealed and threw her arms around her son, hugging him, and kissing him on the cheek. Denny pushed her away, laughing. "Mom. Pack it in, you soppy devil!"

"But that's marvellous Denny. I knew you'd get something soon – and you've always loved doing stuff on the farm. Will you be paid a decent rate?"

"Glyn says that, as I already have some experience of working with the sheep, he'll pay me a little above the minimum wage to start – but he'll review it after three months. If I can take on more responsibility, I'll get more money. In the meantime, I'll be able to give you some money towards my keep."

"That's wonderful news. We'll talk later about how much money you can give me. However, we'll put it in the bank for a couple of months – and it can help pay for your motorbike. What do you reckon?"

"It sounds good to me mom. Thanks."

As Denny laid out cutlery and table mats, Angharad dished out the food. When they had been eating for a few minutes, Denny returned to the motorbike issue.

"I know you don't like driving that old banger of yours for any distance as it's so unreliable and all, but, if I do get a motorbike, mom, you'll be able to ride it too, occasionally. Just think, you could ride into Bangor, or Denbigh, or wherever, and find yourself a boyfriend. I'm sure there are pubs and clubs out there, where you could find yourself a bloke."

"Denny! You are a cheeky bugger at times. If and when I decide I need a man-friend, I'm quite capable of sorting that out myself – and I won't need to go to Bangor or Denbigh. Anyway – my van's fine."

"I'm sorry mom. I realise there are plenty of eligible men around here. I mean, there's Jessie down at the old forge. He's not married, and I know he has an eye for the ladies. He's a bit older than you mind – pushing eighty, I should think."

"Denny!"

"No – then again, I suppose he is a tad wrinkly. What about Dave Roberts? His wife left him last year – and I'm sure he'd love to have a new woman around to help with his kids. All eleven of them. Of course, as he's a coal merchant, he'd also appreciate having a woman about to do the laundry ... " At that moment, Angharad leant across the table, narrowing her eyes and brandishing her fork, mock-menacingly! Denny leant back on his chair. "I'm only trying to be helpful. mom."

Angharad smiled. "To be honest Son, I do sometimes wonder what it would be like to meet up with another man. I've only ever spent any serious time with one bloke, and that was your dad. Sadly, that was an experience that should have put me off men for life. Would you be okay if I did meet another man, though? I mean, it could be tricky. If you didn't get on with him, I'd feel really uncomfortable. Then again – what if he had kids? Would you be able to get along with them? There are so many possibilities. It's all so confusing. Anyway, I'm not sure I'm ready for another man yet. Technically, I'm still married – and I'm still bearing the scars of my time with your dad." Angharad became a little subdued as a torrent of unpleasant memories cascaded over her consciousness.

"Listen, mom. I'll be fine. It's been over two years now since he left and, I for one, hope we'll never see him again. I'm sure you loved him once – but you were always too good for him. He's a revolting man. An animal."

"Okay, Denny. That's enough. I don't want to see him again either – but he is your father." Angharad paused, reflecting. "He did at least give me one worthwhile thing." Denny looked at her questioningly. Angharad smiled back at him. "You!"

After the meal, Denny insisted on tidying up – washing and drying the crocks, as Angharad sat at the table drinking her coffee and watching him beavering away energetically and methodically. She was delighted with her son. His father, Neville, had been an unpleasant and sometimes violent bully who'd often bought terror to the home, particularly if he'd been drinking or taking drugs. He did not often hit Denny, although he did give him the occasional bruise and even gave him a black eye and a bloody nose when Denny once tried to stop him hitting his mother. Angharad was aware that if she, herself, had not gotten into the habit of intervening in disputes between father and son, Denny would almost certainly have suffered significantly. Of course, her interventions inevitably meant that she took the punishments intended for Denny. She still carried the scars – quite literally. An assault with a beer glass resulted in a wound to her left shoulder that required ten stitches. Neville also broke her nose when head-butting her, although, fortunately, the hospital staff were able to reset things effectively. Questions were asked about how she came by those – and many other injuries, and Angharad became adept at lying and making excuses. She doubted, though, whether the doctors and nurses, and even their neighbours really believed that she was clumsy enough to walk into so many doors! She was surprised when Neville left her. She imagined that he'd return before long, but she was more than happy to bask in the relief resulting from his absence. After a few months, she discovered that he'd found work as a gardener and handyman and had left her to move in with his employer, an older American woman who had her own thriving business and a large house about thirty miles away in Caernarfon.

Denny's education, up until that time, had been interrupted frequently as a result of his father's behaviour. Denny was reluctant to attend school while bearing the 'souvenirs' of conflicts with his father, and he was also affected by bouts of stress – resulting mostly from his concerns for his mother. As a result, as long as his father was not at home, he'd spend hours in his room trying to complete homework and other study tasks, when he should really have been at school. When his father was at home, Denny would often sneak out to cycle to the nearby town, where he'd spend the day in a cafe or in the town library. Angharad did her best to encourage him to attend school, but she had to acknowledge that things could be very difficult for him at times – as, indeed, they were for her. When it was apparent that Neville was unlikely to return any time soon, Denny resumed his education with renewed enthusiasm, and he spent an extra year at school, re-sitting exams that he'd failed first time round. Ultimately, he left school with a range of basic qualifications – much to Angharad's delight. Her son had made her proud.

Although she worked full-time, Angharad's job did not pay well, and – even when she worked overtime – she still often struggled to pay the rent and feed Denny and herself. She had a small van, which she used to get to and from work, However, the van was old, unreliable, and had only barely passed its most recent MOT test. On the plus side, she was able to make grocery deliveries locally, and, for that, her boss paid her a premium that helped cover her petrol and insurance costs. All in all, however, Angharad likened her own financial situation to a high wire act. She had at least been able to draw some solace from the fact that Neville was no longer around to leech further money from the family budget. The fact that Denny now had a job, and would be able to contribute a little himself, would help considerably. Angharad felt her mood lift.

Chapter 2

Glyn Edwards stood at the kitchen sink rinsing his mug. It was a warm evening, the window was open, and he could hear chickens clucking and squawking as they scratted in the yard outside. He could also hear ewes bleating on the nearby hillside. He then became aware of an altogether different sound – the clinking of crocks and utensils being washed and stacked in the kitchen next door, as his sister, Carys, and her husband, Jason, cleared up after their meal, in their half of the farmhouse. Before long, there might also be a child next door – a nephew or a niece, and the place would be busier still.

As he looked out across the yard, Glyn's mind drifted back to his early childhood on Anglesey, and the time a few years later when – as his parents were struggling in vain to cope with their own lives – his sister Carys and he came to live with their grandparents at Tan-y-Bryn. He recalled noisy conversations over meals in the very kitchen in which he now stood. There were four living in the house at that time, although it sometimes seemed like fourteen! He smiled as he recalled his gran lifting a blob of soap suds from the sink before placing it carefully – and ceremoniously – on the end of his nose. He remembered her words. "With this blob of suds, I pronounce you 'Sir Glyn of Tan Y Bryn'." He was about eight years old and his sister was five.

Glyn's gaze was then drawn to that single, lonely looking, mug on the drainer. Although he sometimes went round next door to share meals with Carys and Jason, it would be nice to have someone else to chat with in his own kitchen at mealtimes.

He was jolted from his daydream as he caught sight of Jason walking down the short path to Glyn's front door. Jason knocked the door, just as Glyn opened it.

"Hi Jason. Come in."

"Actually, Glyn, we were hoping you'd come round to ours. I've been transferring the wedding video and honeymoon photos to a laptop and Carys wants to know if you'd like to see them." Jason winked. "We've also got a few bottles in the fridge, which I suppose could supplement the impact of the photos – should you be having any problems with insomnia."

"Ha! From what Carys has already told me about your time touring Europe, I can't imagine the photos will be boring."

A short while later, Glyn, was sitting on the sofa in Jason and Carys's living room, with Jason's laptop perched on a small table in front of him. Carys and Jason sat either side of him. Carys suggested that he should scroll through the holiday pictures first, some of which were taken using Jason's digital camera and others taken with either Carys's or Jason's phone. There were pictures taken of – and from – the Eiffel Tower, Notre Dame, The Sacre Coeur Basilica, The River Seine and lots of other touristy places in Paris. However, there were also photos featuring Carys and Jason in 'off the beaten track' attractions such as The Catacombs, and the canals. There were similar series of photos featuring other capital cities including Berlin, Rome and, finally, London. The couple had been away for just three weeks and Glyn was astonished at just how much they'd managed to squeeze in. However, the most impressive aspect of the photos were the images of Carys and Jason themselves. It might be expected that, as honeymooners, they'd look happy. However, on almost every picture, both Carys and Jason looked gleeful, exuberant, or simply jubilant. Yes – that was it, 'jubilant', as in triumphant.

One of the pictures featured the couple standing on the Champs Elysees with the Arc de Triumph in the background. It seemed almost symbolic, a representation of their success. Jason, dressed casually, but – as ever – stylishly, stood with his arm draped around Carys's shoulder. They leant towards each other, smiling broadly at the camera. Carys's long brown hair was being ruffled by the breeze, somehow adding to a sense of carefree joy. Their courtship had been an awfully bumpy ride for both. But, ultimately, they'd won! And, it was so incredibly heart-warming to see.

Glyn said, "That photo is a corker. You should frame it."

The wedding video was fairly short, covering just the key moments from the ceremony and reception. There were, however, quite a few photographs of the wedding. The group photos were of particular interest and viewing them turned into something of a naming contest, as Jason tried to remember the names of Carys's friends and family, and Carys and Glyn tried to recall Jason's.

At one point, Jason said, "There's Jaydee and Claudia from the Village Inn; there's Phil from the garage, and there's that guy who was giving the bride away. Her brother, in fact. What's his name? Erm ... Gilbert ... Graham ...? No – it's glamourous Glyn. Look at those stunning threads!" Glyn had previously described Jason's fashionable clothing as 'threads', and Jason mimicked him. All three laughed. "And there's Glyn's favourite lady, Pattie." Jason paused. "Come to think of it, Glyn, I haven't seen Pattie of late. Where is she?"

Glyn now looked a little downcast. "Well, I did think at one stage that we had a future together – but things have gone off the boil and we've decided on a sort of trial separation. There's no nastiness involved, or anything like that – but it seems we're not really compatible."

"That's a surprise. You've been spending a lot of time together and you seem to get on really well."

"Pattie is lovely – but, to be honest, Jason, it's almost as if she's looking for a husband who will share slipper fetching duties with her. She seems to want to sit by the fire whenever we're at home. A date usually involves a meal at her place, maybe a short walk, and then watching television. She doesn't seem to want to go out anywhere, not even to the pub."

Jason smiled and then apologised. "Sorry Glyn. I have an image of you in fluffy slippers sucking on a clay pipe. I realise though, it's not really all that funny, and I can see how you're concerned."

"I know I'm not a teenager anymore, Jason, but I feel that, at 36, I'm not yet ready to slip into my dotage. I've still got some living to do."

"I can understand that. Have you thought perhaps about going away together? Maybe an activity break or something like that?"

"I considered that and I did suggest to Pattie that we go over to Ireland for a few days, with a view to doing some walking – around the coasts, or a mountain or two. However, she made it clear that she'd much prefer a poolside hotel break. I confess that doesn't really appeal to me."

"Perhaps she's keen to see you take a bit of a rest break, given how hard you work around the farm."

"Yes. I guess you may well be right. I can't help thinking though that Pattie is just not cut out to be a farmer's wife, and I'm not sure I could ever be anything other than a farmer. It's what I do. It's what I am. Pattie is happy managing the café in Betws, and I certainly can't blame her for that. She says she simply can't compete with the demands of the farm. A couple of weeks back, I cancelled a date after I'd asked the vet round to take a look at a ewe that had developed a major limp. It turned out to be nothing of particular concern, but Pattie was unimpressed. She howled down the phone at me, 'I'm sure you love those sheep more than you do me'. She resents the fact that she cannot see me whenever she wants."

At this point, Carys, who'd been listening quietly, spoke up. "I've always liked Pattie. She's warm, and friendly but, in truth, not very interesting. She reminds me of Gavin, that chap I went with for a while before I got together with Jason. Gavin was about as exciting as a wet Wednesday in Wolverhampton. I guess Pattie is similar."

Carys was a little taken aback when Glyn said, "Come on, Carys. That's a bit unfair." Then he smiled – a little ruefully – and added, "Wet Wednesdays in Wolverhampton are not that bad – at least the pubs are open!" He laughed, and said, "Anyway. I think the video and the photos are great. I get the impression that you two are very happy together – even after six whole weeks of marriage!"

Jason smirked, and Carys lifted an empty cider bottle!

♥♥

Jason and Carys had married in August and had toured Europe just as the busy holiday period was easing off. At that time of year, it was fairly quiet on the farm, although ewes, the female sheep, had to be sorted for tupping. Tupping involves mating with a ram, but only those ewes that are old enough and sufficiently healthy are considered suitable. Although Glyn was capable of determining which ewes to 'tup', separating them from the flock was a demanding task and he'd taken on a 17-

year-old called Denny, to help out. Denny had worked on the farm during the summer school holidays for the previous two years and had proved to be bright and energetic with a natural gift for working with sheep. And, just as important, he was reliable. Having Denny on hand when Carys was on honeymoon was a great help – particularly when sheep needed to be gathered. Glyn found that Denny picked up new skills quickly, and he had formed an effective working bond with the farm's border collie, Mollie.

The farm business at Tan Y Bryn was changing. Carys was keen to develop holiday lets on the farm, and she and Glyn had already bought two second hand mobile shepherd's huts and they hoped to buy at least another two, preferably new ones. As they already had a stone-built hut, they'd then have at least five units in all, which they aimed to make available by the following summer. Of course, bringing mobile huts onto the farm sounds simple. However, in practice, it was anything but, and, even after planning permissions were acquired, the practicalities of siting, and the planning and establishment of services – electricity, water, and sewage had to be sorted out, before the huts could be moved into position. Fortunately, Jason, who was a self-employed solicitor and contract writer, was keen to involve himself in the venture when time allowed, and he was also investing financially. When Carys and Jason had returned from honeymoon, Glyn had talked to them about taking Denny on as a full-time farmhand. They all agreed that such a move made good sense, especially as they also planned to explore the development of side-lines such as ewes' milk, cheese production and perhaps even a farm shop.

♥♥

Glyn and Denny had been stacking a few bales of hay onto a trailer attached to the all-terrain vehicle that Denny used to move about the farm. Glyn was impressed with the lad's commitment to his work and he felt it important to acknowledge the fact.

"You seem to be enjoying the work Denny, and you're doing a good job. I'll have a chat with my sister about upping your wages a little bit – so, if you do see Carys about, smile and tell her that she's looking radiant."

"Really?"

"No. On reflection, just smile. Forget the radiant bit. She's old enough to be your mom, and she's married to the guy standing behind you."

Denny swung round to find himself face-to-face with Jason, Carys's husband.

"Hello Jason."

"Hi Denny. Don't listen to Glyn. I know he's your boss – but he doesn't have your best interests at heart." Denny flushed as Glyn laughed. Jason continued. "Seriously, Denny, how's it all going?"

"It's great, thanks. It's nice to have a steady job and to be earning some regular money. I'm hoping to buy a motorbike soon, so I can get to and from home more easily – especially as the winter comes."

"That makes sense. It should give you a bit more freedom and flexibility." Jason pointed towards the turbines on the hill beyond the farmyard. "You'll also be able to use it fetch the odd ewe down from the top of the hill. You'll have to learn how to strap the beggars over the fuel tank first, though."

Denny looked mystified, and he turned towards Glyn, who said, "Don't listen to Jason, Son. He really doesn't have your best interests at heart."

As Glyn and Jason stood giggling, Denny climbed aboard the ATV, waved, and drove off.

Jason turned to Glyn. "I get the impression that the lad is doing all the right things, Glyn."

"To be honest Jason, he's an absolute gem. He learns quickly, and he works his socks off. You probably heard me talking about giving him a raise."

"I've seen him arriving on his bicycle, but where does he come from?"

"He lives a couple of miles outside Llanrwst, which is a fair way off. He has a neighbour who sometimes gives him a lift in his pickup. Denny can put his bike in the back, so he has it available to ride home. I reckon a motorbike would be good for him, though, at least until he's had driving lessons and can buy a car."

"This is not really any of my business, but here's a thought. Might it be possible to help him out with a motorbike? I mean, you could perhaps reduce his raise and put the money towards a motorbike for him. Obviously, it wouldn't have to be a new one."

"That sounds like a cracking idea. We could buy the bike and let him have it on a sort of lease-purchase arrangement. We'll hold back part of his raise and then, after a few months, we'll just hand him the log book."

"By the way, Glyn – and changing the subject – the builders will be here in a couple of days to start work on the new office. They reckon it'll probably take about three days to take the internal wall down and replace the ceiling, and another ten days or so to fit the place out and decorate."

"That sounds good, and a bit quicker than we expected."

"I've been giving some thought to furnishing it all and I'm aiming to set things up so that my desk will face the window. In addition to having a nice view, it should allow us space to introduce a couple of extra chairs, perhaps folding ones, when we have meetings to discuss farm business. How does that sound to you?"

"I reckon that will be great, Jason. It will feel a bit more business-like than trying to squeeze everyone into my lounge, or yours – especially if we have others involved, such as Denny."

"Yes, the more formal setting will suit my business too, especially when entertaining customers or reps. I confess that I feel more comfortable carrying out work tasks away from the living space at home." Jason grinned, as he added, "I must admit that I struggle to focus when I can smell food being prepared in the kitchen."

Glyn went back to the house thinking about how quickly things were moving on the farm. Converting the old dairy-cum-toolshed to the rear of Jason and Carys's half of the farmhouse was a masterstroke. At present, the building was simply used for storing a few pieces of rarely used equipment and other items of junk. A relatively low-cost building job would turn it into a useable and potentially valuable space.

The initial idea for the office had been Jason's and, although he'd no doubt be making most use of it for his own contract writing activities, it would be of great benefit to the farm business, too. Glyn reflected that, in the past, Carys and he had tended to be responsible for the development of the business, but, more recently, Jason had bought a fresh perspective to bear at Tan-y-Bryn farm generally. Glyn had always believed that a business's most important resources were its people, and Jason's input certainly added weight to that idea.

Glyn had spent an hour or so on his laptop, trying to find out what sort of motorbike might be best for Denny. However, the situation regarding engine sizes, driving licences and driver training seemed to be quite complex. Eventually, he gave up, thinking he'd speak to Denny himself, before taking any further steps. He switched off his laptop and headed for the village inn.

As Glyn entered the bar, he nodded to one or two of the regulars there and he also noticed a young man called Eric who worked at the local garage where Glyn normally had his Land Rover serviced. He was aware that Eric rode a motorbike, albeit a relatively powerful one. Significantly, Eric's glass was almost empty.

"Hi Eric. Can I get you a refill?"

"That's very good of you Glyn."

Glyn collected the drinks and joined Eric. "Actually Eric, I have to confess that I'm after something in return."

"Oh yes. What's that then?"

"I'd like to pick your brains on the issue of motorbikes. I'm looking to buy one – preferably a second-hand one – for Denny, the lad who works on the farm. He's only a youngster and this would be his first motorbike. The problem is I have no idea what sort might suit him."

"Will he be using it to ride around the farm?"

"I rather doubt it. He currently tootles about on an ATV."

"That's just as well, as you really need special gearing on a farm bike, especially if it's going to be ridden up and down steep hills. Coincidentally, my younger brother, Grady, has just bought himself a rather snazzy, and powerful, Yamaha. He's got a couple of other bikes, which he's about to put up for sale. One of those might be what you're after. It's a Honda 125. It's not exactly a rocket machine, but it will at least get him started. It does look quite racy, mind, with a fairing – but it should be ideal for a beginner. It was Grady's first bike."

"That could be just the job. What sort of money are we looking at?"

"I'm not too sure. I'm guessing he'd accept about £400 for it. I'll let you have his number – and you can give him a call."

Late the following afternoon, Glyn caught up with Denny, just as he was about to leave for home on his bicycle.

"Hi Denny. How would you like a lift home? I'm going your way."

"That'll be great, Glyn. I'm struggling to cope with the hills, these days. It must be my age!" He grinned.

"Oh yes. I guess, at seventeen, you are becoming quite elderly, and almost 'over the hill'." Denny lifted his bike into the back of the Land Rover, and a short while later, they set off. Glyn told Denny that he was going to take a slight detour.

"There's a chap in the village here who has just bought himself a new motorbike – a powerful Yamaha apparently. He has a couple of other bikes and he's selling his Honda 125." Denny's expression shifted from nonchalance to curiosity. Glyn continued. "I was wondering whether it might suit you. I mean, given that you're growing old and creaky and struggling to stay upright on that pushbike of yours."

"Oh right. I guess I deserved that. The problem is I don't have the money for a motorbike."

"Let's tackle that issue when we come to it."

Grady had bought the motorbike out onto the front driveway of his house and he'd obviously been polishing it, as it sparkled in the early evening sunlight. Glyn hoped that Denny was as impressed with it as he was, as he said, "That looks good. I've half a mind to buy it for myself."

Tearing his attention away from the shiny black and orange machine before him, Denny grinned and said, "Half a mind, eh?"

"Don't go there Denny. Another word, and my wallet stays in my back pocket."

"I'm sorry Glyn – but I don't understand."

"Grady here wants £380 for this. I'm happy to buy it for you. You can then pay me back at £10 a week. I'll take it out of the raise we're about to give you. That is – if you want the motorbike."

Denny looked awe-stricken. "Wow, Glyn. That's brilliant. Thanks."

"Obviously, you'll have to sort out insurance and all that – but if you need any money for that, let me know."

Chapter 3

That evening, Angharad was surprised to see that her son was home before her, and he'd already laid the table ready for them to eat the fish and chip supper that Angharad brought home every Wednesday.

"You're back early, Son. No problems, I hope."

"Hardly. I finished a bit earlier than usual, and Glyn gave me a lift."

When Denny told his mother about the motorbike, she was both delighted and astonished. "Crikey, Denny – that's some employer you've got there. He really looks after you. I reckon he takes better care of you than your own father ever did. Make sure you don't let him down."

"Don't worry about that mom. I won't. He's a nice bloke. Also – in case you're interested, he's not married."

"Denny! Don't start that again." Denny giggled. However, his mom's curiosity was piqued. "How old is this boss of yours, anyway?"

"I'm not sure. About your age, I'd say. So quite old, really."

"You might want some help with money to tax and insure your motorbike – so behave yourself! Seriously, though, why isn't he married, given that he's such a 'nice bloke'?"

"I'm not sure. He said that he was almost married once, years ago, but it all went pear-shaped at the last minute. He didn't tell me any more than that. I know he used to have a girlfriend. I met her when I worked at the farm last summer, but I haven't seen her about lately though."

As the pair continued to eat, Angharad continued to wonder about Denny's employer and about her son's future prospects. He certainly appeared to be enjoying his job at the farm and it seemed that Glyn, his boss, was treating Denny like a proper full-time employee, rather than just a casual farmhand. What Denny said next, reinforced that impression.

"Oh, by the way, Mom – I'm probably going to be home a bit late tomorrow. There's going to be a meeting at the farm, and Glyn's asked me to attend."

"That's interesting. What sort of meeting?"

"Well, as you know, Glyn and his sister Carys own and manage the farm, and Carys's husband, Jason, is also involved. Anyway, they're starting to diversify, and they're buying huts for hire to holiday makers and the like, and they're also talking about introducing a few different sheep breeds as there's a growing market for local wool, sheep's milk and cheese. The meeting is to plan for the future. Glyn says that I'm part of it all now, and he feels I need to know what's happening. He also says that I might be able to contribute ideas to the meeting, as well."

"Blimey, Denny. You're an executive. Before long, you'll be riding around the farm on that quad bike, wearing a suit and tie – and a bowler hat!"

"Mom! Pack it in. This is serious stuff."

"I know, Denny. I'm sorry. I think it's absolutely great, the way things are moving ahead for you. Angharad was quiet for a while and then, as she reflected on the past, and, especially on recent developments, her eyes began well up. She lifted her hand and casually wiped away the tears, but Denny had noticed.

"Mom? Are you okay? What's the matter?"

"I'm fine Denny. Just angry with myself, I suppose."

"What do you mean?"

"It's wonderful the way that things are changing for you now. I've always known that you were bright and hard-working. I reckon, if your father hadn't been such a pain, you'd have ended up at university or something. It seemed that sometimes, he was jealous of what you were doing. I remember when you got good school reports, he'd just make jokes about them, saying your teachers must all have been daft. He never once encouraged you. I should have done more to stop Neville. I let you down."

Denny turned and pulled a sheet of paper towelling from a roll on the worktop behind him. Handing it to his mother, he said, "It's different now Mom. He's gone. We've got to look to the future. Both of us."

"Maybe – but I should have reported him to the police on several occasions – but I was scared of what he'd do. I was afraid that the coppers would just give him a talking to and then send him home. He'd have killed me, and maybe you too. Perhaps I should have tried to get my sister in Chester to let you live with her – out of Neville's way."

"It's not your fault, mom. Stop blaming yourself. I was just as bad. Terrified of him. I sometimes wish that I had the guts to shove him down the stairs when he came home drunk or drugged up. I could have done."

"No Denny. If you had done, what do think your dad would've done when he woke up. He'd have gone berserk."

"Maybe I should have made sure he didn't wake up, by bouncing a hammer over his head."

"Oh, that would have been really clever. I'd have had a dead psycho for a husband, and a murderer for a son. No, Denny, you did well by me. You held it together for both of us." Denny nodded, though looking far from satisfied. His mother stood, walked around the table, and hugged him. "Anyway, he's gone now – hopefully out of our lives forever." Even as she spoke, Angharad experienced a nagging uncertainty. Forever was a long, long time. After all, even though it had been almost two years since she'd last seen Neville, she was still married to him.

Chapter 4

Within about three weeks, Denny had a provisional licence and had completed a basic motorcycle training course. Having access to a motorbike had an immediate, and substantial, impact on several aspects of Denny's life. Getting to and from work was much simpler and he was also able to see his girlfriend Lisa, who lived in Betws-y-Coed, much more often. Glyn noticed, too, that Denny was even more cheerful than normal, since becoming 'mobile'. In an area like southern Snowdonia, personal independence was often linked to having your own 'wheels' – either a car or a motorbike. For a seventeen-year-old like Denny, such independence was especially important.

Denny had attended two meetings at the farm, both of which involved Glyn, Carys, and Jason. All three were aware of Denny's enthusiasm, but they were, nevertheless, astonished by some of the ideas he came up with for potential business developments. For example, after Carys had suggested opening a farm shop, Denny suggested that it might be helpful to contact local schools, both primary and secondary, to see if any of them might be interested in bringing groups of pupils to the farm.

"The younger kids at primary would probably be interested in seeing the animals up close, especially the smaller lambs. Perhaps we could arrange for the children to help with feeding. We could ask the local papers to come in to take pictures. It would help with advertising the business – although the shop would probably need to be up and running, first."

Carys's eyes lit up. "That's a brilliant idea Denny. Thanks for that."

Denny had obviously been giving the issue some thought before the meeting and he had more to say. "The secondary school kids might be interested in learning about how to get into farming. I mean, it's changing all the time, and they might find it helpful to know about the courses they can take after leaving school."

Jason chipped in at this point. "Nice one, Denny. Any other ideas?"

"Only that, if we can get the local paper to pick things up, we could try to promote the holiday huts side of things – although, given that locals will probably not be renting them, I suppose the website is the best way to do that, as long as it's kept up to date."

Glyn now added, "I hope you realise, Denny, that you're generating a lot of work for yourself here."

Denny looked a little alarmed. "Eh?"

Glyn, Jason and Carys, all laughed. Denny was becoming very much a part of the team.

A fortnight later, Denny was asked to attend a further meeting which was called to report on recent developments.

However, at the beginning of the meeting, Carys spoke directly to Denny.

"Denny. We're all aware that you've been working very hard around the farm, getting stuck into almost every aspect of the business, from checking over the ewes to repairing the water supply system in the lambing shed. We've been talking about upgrading your job role. That will involve a salary increase, although, at this stage it will be a modest raise. Now, before I go into more detail, are you okay with that, in principle?"

"Wow, Carys. That sounds great. I don't really know what to say."

Glyn couldn't resist chipping in with, "That'll be a first!"

Jason added, "Ignore him Denny. He's just jealous as he's not getting a raise."

Denny then added, "And he doesn't really have my best interests at heart, does he Jason?"

Carys bought the meeting to order. "Will you all please behave – you're like a bunch of hooligans! Now, Denny – we'd like you to take on key additional responsibility for some aspects of the business, including managing the environment. That will include monitoring, and reporting on the need for repairs to the enclosures, the buildings, the ATVs, and other equipment. I'd also like you to spend some time helping me to develop the business website – especially as you're keen to see it maintained. We've also decided that you'd benefit from some further training at college, focusing on both livestock care and business management. You and I can carry out some research online to see what's available – as long as you're okay with that." By this point, Denny was nodding like a manic apple bobber and grinning from ear to ear.

When Carys said that Denny's new job title would be Assistant Farm Manager, Junior Trainee, and that he'd get a twenty percent salary increase, Denny sat up straight in his chair and muttered, "Bloody hell!"

"Sorry, Denny. What was that?"

"Oh golly, Carys. That's brilliant. Thanks, all of you."

When Denny got home later that evening, he couldn't resist teasing his mother, before telling her of his advancement. "Mom?"

"Yes Denny"

"Do you remember joking about me driving around the farm wearing a suit and a bowler hat?

"Yes, I do. Why?"

"Where can I buy a bowler …?

Chapter 5

Denny got into the habit of finishing any work with the sheep by about lunchtime on Fridays. He could then spend the afternoon with Carys in the farmhouse, working on the business website and developing additional marketing strategies and materials.

One afternoon, Glyn also came in and the three talked briefly about the increasing workload, especially as work was progressing on planning the farm shop. In addition, a further shepherd's hut was now in position on the farm, making four properties in all available to let, as soon as final fitting out and decoration was complete.

Carys spoke. "There's another issue, Denny, of which you're not aware." Denny looked up from the plans laid out before him, and Carys continued. "I'm pregnant. This means that my workload will change. I'm going to keep working full-time for as long as I can, but I'm afraid I'm going to do much less with the sheep, and will switch my focus to the admin side of the business."

"I can understand that, Carys. Working with ewes can be quite strenuous." Denny thought that Carys was one of the hardest working women he had ever known – but, he acknowledged, even she had her limits.

"I'll still do some work outside, but I'll concentrate on the older and non-pregnant ewes. Working indoors at lambing time can be hazardous for pregnant women, especially during the latter stages of pregnancy. Even handling silage and cleaning potentially contaminated clothing and boots can be dodgy."

Denny was sympathetic, and curious. "That sounds sensible, Carys. I have to confess, though, I didn't know about the risks involved."

"It's likely that you'll get to know more when you take up some training at college. Meanwhile though, we're going to be looking for at least one extra member of staff."

Glyn spoke at this point. "If you know of anyone who could cover some of Carys's work – especially in the lambing shed, then let us know. It wouldn't need to be a skilled herdsman, mind – just someone who doesn't mind a bit of mud and sheep poo, who's keen to learn and who doesn't mind some hard work. Ideally, the person should be able to offer at least three days a week, although, if they're able, we'd offer full-time work – at least until lambing is completed."

Denny thought for a moment. "I might know of someone – but I'll have to get back to you, when I've spoken to them." Denny then turned to Carys and added, "And by the way, congratulations to you and Jason."

The following day, Denny was at work early, driving around the farm, checking all of the perimeter fences. He had enough experience to know that, if there was a hole in a fence, then the sheep would find it. At lunch time, he called into the farmhouse and found Carys at home.

"Hi Carys. I said I might know somebody who could pick up the extra work. I've had a word with her, and she'd like to apply."

"Oh good. You said 'her'. A female?"

"Yes. It's my mom. She does have some experience of farm work, and working in a lambing shed. It's been a few years though, so obviously, you'd have to have a chat with her."

"Do you really think she could cope, Denny?"

"I do – but then, she's my mother, so I guess I'm a bit biased."

"When could she come in to see me?"

"Well, she works in a shop every day except Sunday and Wednesday, but she'd be happy to come in on either of those days, or in the evening."

It was Wednesday, and Carys asked Denny to let his mother know that she'd be happy to see her on Sunday, or on almost any evening.

Chapter 6

It was the morning after Denny had told his mother about the interview at the farm. Angharad had just made a couple of local grocery deliveries, and had returned to the shop. It was always good to get away from the store – especially when her boss, Mike, was about. She'd worked at the shop for some years, but, even after all this time, Angharad tried to avoid any close contact with him – he had always had wandering hands and, if anything, his behaviour had become worse of late. It would soon be lunchtime, so she'd be able to get out again for a 30-minute break. However, as she busied herself topping up some of the shelves, she began to wonder what it would be like to swap the dark, almost stifling interior of the minimarket – which had small windows, tall shelves and inadequate lighting – for the wide outdoors on a farm. Okay – working at the farm might be challenging at times, especially during the winter months, but it would certainly be preferable to her current existence. It was a challenge she was prepared to take on, even though she'd be swapping a permanent job for one which guaranteed only short-term employment. Also, of course, she hadn't got the job yet. She'd have to give it her all at interview!

In the event, Angharad arranged to drive to the farm on the following Sunday.

Although both Jason and Glyn were away in South Wales looking at the potential purchase of additional huts for their fledgling letting concern, having Angharad visit during the day meant that Carys could interview her informally, and then show her around the farm – if it appeared that she could handle the work.

♥♥

Denny offered to go to the farm with his mother, but Angharad was uneasy about that. She said to Denny that it would feel as if she, herself, were being 'shepherded' and she did not want Denny's presence to put undue pressure on Carys Edwards to take her on. As she pulled up outside the farmhouse in her old van, Carys came out to meet her. It had been a while since Angharad had last been interviewed for a job, and she felt rather nervous. However, Carys's warm greeting helped to put her mind at ease.

"Hello there. You must be Angharad. Denny has told me a lot about you. I'm Carys."

"Hi Carys. It's really good to meet you."

"Come inside. I'm just making a coffee, if you'd like one. I can tell you a bit about the job, before I show you around. Will that be okay?"

"That sounds great. Thanks."

The pair were of similar age and slipped comfortably into conversation. Angharad remarked that the house was impressive, although the living arrangements were a bit confusing.

"There seem to be doors everywhere here. It's tricky to see where one house ends and the other one begins."

"Well, as you've probably guessed, this used to be one rather large farmhouse. It was left to Glyn and me by our grandparents. A few years ago, Glyn was about to get married, and we decided to split the house into two parts, so Glyn would have a ready-made family home. Sadly, though, the marriage didn't happen. Anyway – if you don't mind my asking – what about you? Denny told me that you were separated."

"Yes. It's been a couple of years since I last saw Nev, my husband." Angharad looked to the floor and, as she looked up again, she added, "and, no, I don't miss him."

Carys did not pursue the issue, and turned to the subject of work.

"Denny has obviously told you that we're looking for somebody to help out around the farm, especially during lambing, as I'm expecting." Carys patted her tummy as she continued. "I'll be reducing my contact with the sheep as things progress. We'd like someone to do at least three days a week – but we could probably offer full time work, at least in the short term. Denny gave me a brief outline of your circumstances, but he was reluctant to speak for you. Can you tell me a little about what you're doing at present?"

"At the moment, I'm working in a minimarket in the village close to where I live. I've been there for about three years now. It pays the rent – but I have to confess, I've never really enjoyed it. I'm fine with the customers for the most part – but I am starting to find the more routine side of things, such as stacking shelves, cleaning, and sorting and picking stock from the shelves for deliveries, to be quite tedious at times. I accept that though – it's part of the job. However, it doesn't pay well – and the boss can't keep his hands to himself. I know this sounds awful to say, but he's fat and he's ugly and he's married – so I don't find his attention at all flattering."

"Crikey. I don't know about 'awful to say'. It just sounds awful to me. Period! Anyway – changing the subject, I gather you have some experience of farm work?"

"Yes. My parents used to rent a small farm just outside Wrexham. We had a flock of about 60 ewes and I used to help out at lambing time. We also had about a million chickens – or at least that's how it seemed to me at the time."

Carys laughed. "We have a few here, mostly for our own use. They do seem to get everywhere though. Were yours for egg production?"

"Yes. We sold to a few local shops and we also had a Saturday market stall. I keep saying 'we' – but I should point out that I was only in my early teens when my mom left us. She ran off with an animal feed salesman, and soon afterwards, my dad had to let the farm go and we moved to Chester. I also have an older sister who was never really interested in farm work, and she still lives in Chester, but I left there when I got married – more fool me. My dad recently remarried and moved to Liverpool. So, there you go – there's a bit of a family history there, and, obviously, my farming skills are a bit rusty, but I'd love the chance to show you what I can do."

"What I can do is show you around, and you can fire away with any questions that you have."

Carys had fuelled up an ATV and she drove Angharad about, showing her the main pastures and landscape features, including the hilltop turbines and the ravine where sheep sometimes sheltered in bad weather. Angharad began asking questions about where the most productive areas of grass were, how far out and how high the ewes tended to roam, and where extra winter food was usually dropped. After they'd spent about an hour touring the farm, Carys asked Angharad if she'd like to drive the ATV back to the farmyard and, within a few minutes, Angharad's confidence was evident. "I did drive a quad bike some years back. I used to worry about turning it over though, especially on the hills – but this feels a lot more stable than I remember."

"I prefer these to quad bikes. They're also better for moving stuff about the farm, and, of course, they'll carry two people."

When they returned to the yard, Carys asked Angharad to pull up outside of their main lambing shed. As they climbed from the ATV, Angharad looked about, and asked Carys if there was anyone else working at that time.

"No. Denny doesn't normally work on Sundays, of course – and Glyn and Jason are away looking at mobile huts – at least that's what they told me." Carys grinned and rubbed her chin, as she added, "It's funny how these relatively simple trips involve a stop-over."

Angharad interrupted, "A boys' night out?"

"Exactly."

As they entered the shed, Angharad stood for a moment and looked around with something close to awe. The shed was so much bigger, more modern, brighter, and cleaner than the one she remembered on her parents' farm. She spent a few seconds struggling, at first, to take everything in. Tan Y Bryn was simply different.

Carys interrupted her thoughts. "You're probably aware of this, but the vast majority of the in-lamb ewes – those that are pregnant – are brought into the shed before giving birth, so that they can be monitored and fed more effectively. We also need to ensure that their health is monitored. For example, foot-rot can be an issue at this time of year, especially indoors. We have a couple of ewes in here now – in fact, Denny brought them in yesterday, so I could demonstrate moving them about, and show you how we check for diseases."

Carys led Angharad to a nearby pen containing two sheep. There was a frame fixed to one wall of the pen. It was tilted at an angle of about 45 degrees and was fitted with some strong rope netting. Angharad had never seen such a device before, although she had seen something similar on a beach. "That looks like a deck chair. I know sheep like to laze on occasion, but … "

"Actually, it really is called a deck chair. I'll show you how it works." Carys caught the smaller ewe and, holding its head, she backed it up to the chair and its momentum helped her to flip it over onto its back, so that it lay in the webbing. "You can see that it makes trimming the feet, tagging the ears and medicating them much easier. You don't really have to hold the ewe in position – which makes everything much easier. If the ewe is particularly energetic, there are straps you can use to hold her down.

Angharad had never used such a chair and said, "That looks a whole lot simpler than turning them onto their sides by hand, although I have done that in the past."

"Would you like to have a go now?"

"Sure. Why not." Angharad had deliberately worn jeans and boots in preparation for her visit. She took off her jacket, and stepped into the pen with Carys and the two ewes. She managed to move the larger ewe to the deck chair and, after an initial struggle, she pushed the animal backwards into the device, so that it was lying on its back at an angle with its hooves easily accessible. Angharad inspected the hooves, announcing that they seemed generally fine, although one of the hooves looked as if it had been damaged. Carys was very impressed.

"Well spotted, Angharad. That ewe has had a problem with the hoof. We spotted it yesterday and we'll keep it inside for a while, for treatment and monitoring.

"Actually, Carys, I'm surprised at how comfortable I am with all this at the moment. I know the whole industry has changed – but the sheep haven't, I guess. Can I try to roll the other one over?"

"Go for it. Take care though. If you've not done this for a while, you could easily pull a muscle or something."

Angharad stepped to the smaller ewe and reached over it, before grabbing its legs and pulling it on to its side. Apart from a touch of grunting and puffing, she managed well. Carys placed her hands on her hips and adopted a quizzical expression.

"When did you last do this?"

"Oh – it's probably been almost twenty years now."

"Well, Angharad, you certainly seem comfortable around the sheep." Nodding towards the deck chair, she added, "and the fact that you're not afraid to 'have a go' when using unfamiliar kit is also remarkable. Well done."

Ultimately, Carys was delighted with Angharad's potential. She explained that, if she wanted the job, it was hers.

Angharad grinned, and said, "That's wonderful Carys. I'm really looking forward to starting. I should be able to leave the minimarket after working just a week's notice." Carys, who could sense a little tension in Angharad's voice, gave her a quizzical look, so Angharad elaborated. "The boss's wife has just begun working in the shop and I have a suspicion that she may have heard about his antics: in addition to messing about with me, he has also started to flirt with the latest addition to the staff, a school leaver. I think he'd normally want a fortnight's notice, but I'm guessing that, as he can no longer afford to harass either of us, he'll be quite happy to see me leave a little sooner."

Chapter 7

Tan Y Bryn's new shepherdess, Angharad Lloyd, started work a little over a week later, just as the first few ewes had been brought into the shed for lambing. Denny spent a while with his mother to ensure that she was able to cope without too much difficulty. As Angharad got stuck into her role and became more comfortable, Denny left the shed for short periods to check on other livestock around the farm. Angharad had seen Carys, but had yet to meet Jason, who was visiting his own clients in the West Midlands, and she had not yet seen Glyn who had left the farm early to travel to Ruthin, where, apparently, he hoped to pick up a few extra panels with which to construct additional holding pens in the shed.

Shortly before midday, Angharad was in the shed monitoring the progress of a small number of early lambing ewes. She was relieved that things were going smoothly at this early stage of her employment, although she knew that she could run across to the house to ask Carys's advice, should she encounter any problems. She'd been interrupted a little earlier as Carys called her out of the shed to introduce her to a small group of primary age children and a couple of teachers. They were keen to know about lambing, and Carys listened in as Angharad gave the group a brief overview of the process.

"Unfortunately, you're here a bit early, as there's only one new born lamb in the shed, although we expect to see lots more in the next few days." Angharad showed the children around the shed and fielded questions in an appropriately child-friendly manner." As the group left, Carys winked at Angharad and gave her the 'thumbs 'up'. She was evidently happy with Angharad's approach.

A few minutes later, the noise of the group's chatter had dissipated, and, as Angharad moved away from the ewes, she turned towards the door of the shed and noticed a man watching her. He was dressed in casual, but fairly tidy clothes, and she assumed he was a visitor – probably another teacher.

She said, "Oh hello. You shouldn't really be in here unaccompanied. You'll find the boss in the yard. If she's not out there, you could try knocking on that red door over there." Angharad pointed towards Carys's front door.

The man made to interrupt. "Oh, well…"

"Look, I'm sorry – but this sheep is about to lamb, and she is struggling a bit…"

"Well – as long as you think you can handle it…I'll tootle off and leave you to it."

"I'm sure I'll manage…oh…!"

The man was halfway across the yard as Angharad finished speaking. She experienced a sudden moment of doubt …

A few minutes later, the man returned, accompanied by Carys, who remained close to the shed door, away from the ewes.

As Angharad looked up from the sheep, Carys spoke first. "Hi again, Angharad. I gather that you've met my brother, Glyn."

Angharad looked from Carys to Glyn – who was grinning, inanely.

"Bugger. Sorry. You should have said."

Still grinning, Glyn responded. "I tried, but I couldn't get a word in. Anyway, you seemed to be coping – so I thought I'd leave you to it. Having said that, you should try to keep cold drafts at bay by closing the shed doors – especially in this weather – as new-born lambs are at risk of hypothermia."

"Oh sorry. If and when, the lamb appears, I'll be sure to close the doors."

"Maybe – as long as you're not distracted by other issues, such as another ewe struggling to deliver her lamb. I'm sorry to badger you – but it's important to plan ahead where you can. Both Carys and I have done this a good few times and I'm sure that my sister will confirm that it's easy to be overtaken by events when lambing kicks off in earnest." Glyn glanced back at Carys, who, unsurprisingly, seemed reluctant to engage with what was becoming a fractious discussion. Glyn left the barn, adding, "Anyway, Angharad – welcome to Tan Y Bryn. If you learn half as quickly as your son, you'll be fine."

♥♥

As Glyn walked across the yard towards the house, he heard Angharad say to Carys, "Blimey – he does go on a bit!" While he acknowledged that she'd only been on the farm for a short while, Glyn was not entirely comfortable with Angharad's approach.

The following day, Glyn went over the hill to gather together, and herd, a small flock of heavily pregnant ewes back down to the shed. He took the farm's sheepdog, Molly, and Denny also went with him on Glyn's ATV. Glyn had bought ATVs after Carys had a serious accident on the farm when she drove her quad bike into a ravine. In addition to being safer than quad bikes, the ATVs carried two people and more equipment than quads. As they approached the ewes, Denny mentioned that his mother had told him about her meeting with Glyn. As he turned to Denny, Glyn narrowed his eyes and said, "And what exactly did your mom tell you?"

Denny giggled and said that she'd described Glyn as a bit strict.

"And what else did she say?"

"Well…"

"Yes? C'mon, Denny. Out with it."

"She says you're a hard-nosed blighter and that you're a bit up yourself."

"That's interesting. Do you know why?"

"No. Why."

"Because that's pretty well how I'd describe her. She certainly doesn't like being told what to do, does she?"

"No. But then she was married to a bloke who used to tell her what to do, and then she'd get used as punchbag if she didn't do exactly as he said. I guess she has learned to defend herself against bullies."

"What? You don't think I'm a bully, do you?"

"No way. And I told my mom that I think you're a great boss, now that I've gotten to know you a bit better."

"Mm! Do you reckon she thinks I'm a bully?"

"No – but I'm sure she'll let you know if you push her too far."

"Okay. I'll bear that in mind. Anyway, shifting focus, let's get these sheep rounded up."

"Fair enough."

"By the way, Denny. You can tell your mom from me, that I reckon she's an awkward, argumentative bugger!"

"Will do."

Chapter 8

Angharad settled into her role at the farm, spending most of her time in the lambing shed. However, she also went out and about, usually with Denny, to place hay at strategic points about the farm. During the colder months, the grass was not re-growing as quickly as it did during the rest of the year, so there was a risk that the ewes that remained outdoors might struggle for nourishment. Denny had grown increasingly knowledgeable about many aspects of sheep farming and was often able to advise his mother about particular issues relating to lambing. In addition, Carys was a reliable source of knowledge, although she generally stayed out of the shed. During the busiest periods, both Angharad and Denny worked very industriously indeed, often remaining at the farm into the late evening. Glyn took what he called the 'overnight shift' and he also helped during the daytime – as long as he could remain awake. Although he often joked when speaking to Denny, Glyn's exchanges with Angharad were more polite. One evening at home, she raised this with Denny.

"Do you think I'm doing okay at the farm, Denny?"

"You seem to be coping really well. Why do you ask?

"Well – it's Glyn. I know he speaks to me, but there's no banter, as there is with you. He seems, well … I don't know really. Formal, I guess. To be honest, he's not all that friendly."

"Mm. I hadn't really noticed. Perhaps he's still trying to weigh you up. I've been trying for seventeen years, and I still haven't figured you out."

"Denny – you're not being very helpful, here."

"I'm sorry, Mom. I don't really know what to say. I suppose you'll just have to be patient. He is a nice bloke really. Give him time."

"I'm sure you're right. We'll see."

Glyn entered the lambing shed as Angharad was tidying up after the last of the lambs had been turned out to pasture. Angharad, supported by Denny, and occasionally Glyn, had engineered what Glyn had described as a 'clean sheet'. Although there had been a small number of 'orphan' lambs – those whose mothers had rejected them, along with one whose mother had unfortunately died whilst birthing, all of the orphans had been matched with ewes that had given birth to just one lamb.

"Hi Angharad. Do you think you'll be finished in here soon? I'd like to clear the floors completely – you know, move all of the hay out, so the place can be hosed down. We can then disinfect it all. This is something I prefer to do after lambing as it helps to ensure good hygiene. Some of the bugs associated with lambing can remain in the environment for a long time."

Angharad had barely heard him. She was aware that, when lambing was over, she might be released from her job on the farm. She had understood from the outset that the role was a temporary one, although she had hoped that perhaps she'd be allowed to stay on, even on a part-time basis. The key moment had arrived – and it stung. She'd worked hard. Very hard. She believed that she'd impressed those around her – Carys, Jason, her son Denny, and maybe even Glyn. Obviously, it was simply not enough. Glyn's words echoed in her head. *Do you think you'll be finished in here soon?* She felt her eyes misting. She took a deep breath before responding.

"When should I finish? Today, or at the end of the week?"

"Eh? Sorry Angharad. What do you mean?"

"Lambing is over. You want me to finish here at Tan Y Bryn."

Glyn was quiet for a moment. He looked slightly confused. You do sometimes make mistakes, Angharad … "

"But I've always done my best Glyn. I'm still learning. It's just … "

"You've made another mistake, Angharad."

"What …"

"You're not being let go, Angharad. At least, not unless you really want to leave."

"I'm sorry Glyn. I don't understand. Perhaps I'm being a bit dim here."

Glyn laughed. "I'll come back to that later. Meanwhile – are you happy to stay at Tan Y Bryn?" Angharad was stunned and could only nod. "Not so long ago, I seem to recall saying to Denny that you were an awkward, argumentative bugger."

"I know. I remember. He told me."

"Well, I still think you're an awkward, argumentative bugger. However, you're a worker, you've learned quickly, and you've done wonderfully well here. You're a real asset to the farm. I've spoken to the team – which includes Denny – and we're all agreed that there's a place for you here on an ongoing basis, if you want it."

"Glyn. That's fantastic. But what will I do, especially now that lambing's finished?"

"Well, to start with, you can help me clear the hay from this place. I'd like to get it all cleaned over the next few hours. Then, we're going to have a planning meeting at my place tomorrow evening. We'll all be there, me, Carys, Jason, Denny, and, ideally, you – if you can make it. We'll start thinking about how best to move forward from this point. Are you okay with that?" Angharad nodded and smiled and, when Glyn stepped forward holding out his hand to shake hers, Angharad touched his hand briefly, before throwing her arms around him.

"Oh Glyn. Thanks. Oh crikey – this means so much to me." As she broke away, she sensed surprise in Glyn's expression. Nevertheless, he smiled back at her.

"Take a break, Angharad. I'll be back in a while." As Glyn turned to leave, Angharad recalled Glyn's earlier comment.

"Oh Glyn. When I said earlier that I was being 'a bit dim', you said you'd return to that issue later. What did you mean?"

"As I said, Angharad – later!"

♥♥

Angharad went into the storage shed next to the main lambing shed. She opened the door and pulled out a folding chair. She had gotten into the habit of sitting there enjoying her lunch, as long as the weather was fine. It was indeed fine, as was, it seemed, just about everything else. She was now a full-time employee at Tan Y Bryn. It felt wonderful. She thought back over the previous weeks, reflecting on what could have been a relatively perilous move from an unpleasant, though reliable job in the minimarket, to become a shepherdess at Tan Y Bryn. She loved the position, and had been dreading leaving. Even Glyn seemed to have softened and was now quite friendly with her, exchanging the odd comment, or jokey insult, and she had begun to joke back. As Denny had said, he was, in truth, a nice bloke. She looked across the yard to the hill beyond. It was bathed in spring sunshine and she could see several ewes with their tiny lambs, many of which she had helped bring into the world. It felt good. Her phone peeped, as a text came through. It was from Glyn.

Hi Angharad. I'm glad you've decided to stay with us here at the farm. As I said, you have been doing a really good job. As for you being dim – well, you're no dimmer than a mole's belly button. I do think you're as yampy as a sack of badgers, mind.

Angharad almost choked on her sandwich. She was tempted to respond in some detail immediately, but she held back. She'd spend some time later composing an appropriate response. For the moment, she simply answered, *Just you wait!*

During the afternoon, Angharad worked with Glyn clearing out the shed. The exchange of texts was not mentioned. There was, however, a new dynamic developing, evident in exchanged comments, smiles, eye contact, and occasional winks.

Denny came into the shed on one occasion to speak to Glyn about some damaged fencing. As he left, he called out to Angharad, who was at the far end of the building. "Hi Mom. Are you okay?"

"Brilliant, Denny. Bloody brilliant!"

Denny glanced back at Glyn, who was grinning.

♥♥

That evening, after tea, Angharad gave Denny an update.

"You were right, Son. Glyn is a nice bloke when you get to know him."

"Oh yes?" Denny raised his eyebrows and smiled, knowingly.

"Denny! He's my boss. He's just given me a full-time job. Like I said, 'He's a nice bloke.' Now don't read anything more into it."

"Yes Mother."

"Denny. Behave!"

Chapter 9

Angharad was beginning to spend more time driving around the farm, checking on the condition of the livestock and occasionally moving feed and equipment about. She had become quite confident on the ATV – and Carys was a little concerned that she could become over-confident. One morning Carys invited Angharad into the house to share a coffee and a chat. Both women found it helpful to exchange ideas, tips, and updates. They were also becoming good friends. Carys commended Angharad on her developing skills before telling her not to become too blasé when driving the ATV, as they could prove dangerous to the unwary.

    Angharad was keen to know more, and said, "Denny said something about you having an accident over the hill a while back." Carys then gave Angharad a rough overview of an accident she'd had at the ravine, and the events that followed it. Angharad was stunned to hear how closely Carys came to death and how Jason ultimately saved the day by rescuing her. "So that's how you finally got together with Jason. Gosh – it sounds like a cross between a nightmare and a fairy story."

    Carys nodded several times. "Oh yes. That's not a bad description. The tale did have a happy ending though." Both women smiled.

"Being a nosy sort, I've noticed that you have some scarring around your knee, and I'm also aware that you carry a slight limp on occasion. Is that something to do with the accident?"

"Exactly. My knee was in a bit of a mess, and it's still a little sore sometimes, especially when the weather gets cold." Carys held up her left hand. "I lost my little finger, and you've probably seen the scarring on the side of my face, too." Carys pulled back her long hair, revealing a faint scar running from her hairline onto the left side of her face. "Happily, I was offered some extra plastic surgery to help reduce the scarring." Carys grinned, and added, "Otherwise, I'd be even uglier that I am now."

"Don't be daft!" Angharad then asked, "How come Glyn isn't married? He's a lovely bloke really. It's a wonder some woman hasn't snapped him up by now. I remember Denny saying that he had planned to get married – but that it didn't happen. Denny didn't know why though."

"Oh, yes. Glyn was close to it a few years back – but, his fiancée was killed in a motor accident just a week before the wedding."

Angharad lifted her hand to her mouth in shock. She remained silent, trying to assimilate everything that she had just learned. She felt compelled to say that the Edwards' family history had certainly had its ups and downs.

Carys continued. "That's a little about my background as an adult, and about Glyn's. What about yours, if you don't mind my asking."

"I don't mind at all, although it's a bit of a helter-skelter tale." Angharad paused, drawing in a breath, before proceeding. "I met Neville when I was 15. He was a bit older at 18. I met him at a fairground where he was working on the waltzers. I suppose I was attracted by his wild, rebellious nature. In truth, he was a bit of a throwback – a rocker with a studded leather jacket and slicked-back black hair. I was in awe of him, I guess. We went out on a few dates and made love several times, including at his house when his parents were on holiday. We also had sex in his mate's caravan – which, I believe was where I got pregnant, shortly after my 16th birthday. We normally relied on condoms but, on that occasion, he didn't have any. He said it wouldn't be a problem as he'd withdraw before he 'came'. Looking back, I'm astonished at how naïve I was at that age. The benefit of hindsight, eh?"

Carys was wide eyed, obviously surprised. "So that was how Denny came into the world?"

"Yes, indeed. We married when Denny was just a few months old. Denny was about the only good thing that Neville gave me. I wasn't entirely comfortable about marrying Neville, as he was developing a taste for alcohol, and he'd also hit me a few times. However, he insisted that Denny needed a father, and he'd also half convinced me that, once we were married, things would be different, as he'd feel less stressed about our relationship. All nonsense of course. That naïveté again."

"You said that Neville left a couple of years ago. How did you cope before that? Did things get any better?"

"I don't recall things getting better generally, although we had patches when life at home was tolerable. He tended to spend periods away from home and he even went back to work with the fairground as it travelled to a variety of places, especially during the summer. By the time Denny went to primary school, I was having to hoard money to buy essentials. Neville was into both booze and drugs and I recall a time when he'd taken all the money we had, to buy stuff to feed his habit. I had to borrow a few pounds from a neighbour so that I could feed Denny. Neville wanted to know where I'd got the money from and, when I told him, he beat me, breaking my nose. I'm not sure, even now, why he did so. Perhaps it was to reduce his own feelings of guilt. One of the worst aspects of the situation was the control that Neville exercised over me. I had to account for my movements, and my spending, and Neville constantly quizzed me about anyone I met – even women. He was mind-numbingly jealous. There were several more violent incidents, some of them even involving Denny. It was no great surprise when he left. As I said, he'd gone off with the fair before. However, when, after a few weeks, he still hadn't returned, I resolved to make the most of his absence and to enjoy life a little more. Then, a couple of months later still, a friend told me that she'd heard that Nev was working for a woman in Caernarvon. Apparently, she's American, and rather wealthy, and Neville was taken on as a gardener and general handyman – which is weird – as he's never been any good at DIY and he also hates gardening. I was amazed by it all, but also relieved to have a break from his nastiness. The last I heard though, was that he'd formed a personal relationship with the woman, and had moved in with her. Good luck to her. I just hope she can take a punch." Angharad paused. "Sorry, Carys – I'm being rather cynical, but it is a relief to be free of him."

"There's no need to apologise. What about Denny? Does he miss his dad?"

"Not in the least. My fear is that, if Neville were to turn up now, Denny would be anything but the loving son – and Denny's much bigger and tougher than he was when Neville left. I just hope things never come to that."

Lambing had ended and, even though she did her best to stay busy, Angharad sometimes began to find herself at a loose end, seeking out additional work at the farm. She began to pick up some of the work that Denny normally covered, such as locating and reporting on breaks in the fencing, damage to shed roofs, and any other maintenance issues that cropped up. This did enable Denny to spend a little more time developing the farm website, which was becoming a key issue as the holiday lets were being furnished, and the farm shop was being sited. At the same time, Denny was helping Carys and Glyn to devise additional potential promotional activities for the business.

Angharad often attended planning meetings in Jason and Carys's office, contributing whenever she felt able. At one mid-summer meeting, initial discussion – led by Jason – focused on the holiday lets. After that, Carys led discussion on the farm shop.

"As you all know, we have a fair-sized area of hard standing laid out, services in place, and four large containers – the 'back end' of the shop – in situ. Glyn has sourced another unit – a second-hand holiday lodge, which should be easy to convert into a shop front. As it stands, that could be installed by the end of the week, and everything connected up in another two weeks or so." She turned to Angharad. "We're using the same builders who converted this place."

Angharad glanced around. "That sound sensible. They did a nice job."

"My concern now, is that things are moving along at a rapid pace, and I can foresee a situation where we have a fully functional building with nothing in it. A shell – but no shop." Carys paused, and, surprisingly, no-one in the group – neither Jason, Glyn, Denny nor Angharad – spoke up. Carys turned to face Angharad. "Any thoughts?"

Everyone's attention now shifted to Angharad who was obviously surprised by the question. "Erm…I'm thinking that I'd like to have a proper look at the inside of the shop, and I'd like to spend some time talking about what's going to go on sale and when. After that, I might be able to make some suggestions." She hesitated, and then added, "if you think that might be of value."

Glyn started giggling. "Angharad. I'm sorry – you've been stitched up!"

"What do you mean?"

"You can blame Denny. He said you were worried about not having enough work to do about the farm. However, we're all aware of the seasonal shifts in sheep farming and we all know that you are no slacker. However, Denny says that you worked at that grocery store from the time it opened, and that you were involved in getting the business off the ground. If you're willing, we'd like you to devote some time to helping Carys to get the shop up and running here."

Carys then added, "You asked if your suggestions might be of value. I'm pretty sure they will be, Angharad."

At the end of the meeting, Angharad agreed to spend some time with Carys the following day. They'd be able to look at the shop facilities that were already in place, and they'd also be able to begin planning beyond that, with a view to identifying a target for the shop opening date.

Chapter 10

Neville Lloyd had been living with middle-aged American widow, Kelly Garcia for almost two years. Kelly had given him a job, allowed him to make love to her and, eventually, she'd taken him into her home. However, the relationship started to break down after a few months, and, since that time, Neville had sponged off her and begun to behave increasingly aggressively toward her – something he'd had plenty of practice at. Ironically, perhaps, although Neville had gradually become more and more unpleasant, Kelly had never been subjected to any real violence. If she'd known more about his history in that respect, she'd have gathered some friends around her, before threatening Neville with legal action if he did not leave her home. When she did order him to leave, Neville beat her severely, knocking one of her teeth out and bruising her face, before locking her in a pantry. He then stole what little money he could find in the house, before taking off in the car that he'd been using, but which actually belonged to her. *My boss, eh? I showed her who's boss. The silly old bag.*

      Neville bought some cans of beer, drove along the coast to Conway and parked the car. After spending an evening in a pub, he purchased more booze, along with a couple of grams of weed. He returned to the car and, after drinking and smoking into the early hours, he nodded off. He woke early, shivering and hungry. He had only a small sum of money remaining in his pockets – he couldn't remember where he'd spent the rest. He walked to a café and had some breakfast. Then, after eating, he complained to the manageress that the beans had been cold, and he asked for his money back. The manageress was unsympathetic.

"It's a bit late to be asking for a refund. If you'd have told me the beans weren't warm enough, I'd have put your plate in the microwave and heated it up for you."

"So, you're not going to give me my money back then? You dish out shit food, and you expect to get away with it."

"I'm not trying to get away with anything. I'm not used to people complaining – and I do my best to provide good food. I'm sorry you're not happy with what you got."

At this point, the morning-after effects of beer and weed kicked in as Neville – unwisely – started to shout. "You're darned right, I'm not happy – you fucking slapper!" As two rather beefy-looking lorry drivers rose from their table and moved in his direction, Neville left.

Neville's mind, which was hardly the most effective instrument at the best of times, was now in utter turmoil. What should he do? He had found only a little money after thumping Kelly and leaving her locked in the pantry – and that money was now almost all gone. He couldn't go back to Kelly's as she'd been expecting guests, and they'd certainly have been able to hear her shouting – as the pantry had an air vent on an outside wall. They'd have called the police, and the police would no doubt be on the lookout for him. Where could he go?

He drove around for a while and then headed away from the coast. A while later, he arrived at the house where he and his wife Angharad had lived. He desperately needed some money.

Neville knocked the door, but there was no answer. He went round to the back of the house, hoping to find the spare key which had always been kept under a plant pot by the shed. *Damn!* The plant pot was no longer there and he paced about the yard lifting rocks and other pots – anything that might conceal the key. Finally, frustration overcame caution and he lifted a stone from a small rockery adjacent to the patio. He needed a good few heavy whacks to penetrate the double glazing on the back door, but, after a minute or so, he was inside. As he entered, he found it easy to justify his actions to himself. *Angharad is still my wife – so this is still my house. Sort of.*

Neville wanted money for booze and for drugs. He turned out drawers and wardrobes – even Denny's – and rummaged through the kitchen, and downstairs cupboards, without success. There was no money, although he did find a small laptop computer in Denny's room. Again, justification came readily. *That kid owes me. I was always buying stuff when he was little. This should fetch me a few bob at the pawnshop or down the pub.*

Neville raided the fridge, and stuffed a small pork pie into his mouth, washed down by two bottles of cider. Still, there was no money to be found. He then noticed an unfamiliar earthenware jar in the corner of the kitchen worktop. He lifted it and it rattled. *Money! How much is in here?* Neville pulled off the lid and emptied the contents onto the worktop. There were plenty of coins – but all were of low denomination, 1p and 2p, with the occasional 5p piece thrown in. The whole lot would barely add up to a couple of pounds. *Bitch!* He hurled the jar across the kitchen smashing it against the tiled wall behind the sink. He screamed, "Where's the fucking money? She owes me loads – all the stuff I bought her in the past." Neville strode into the living room, his fury mounting. He became aware of the new and improved decor. She'd made changes since he was last in the house almost two years before. There was a new sofa, new wallpaper and new curtains. Then, he homed in on several candles, on the mantelpiece and on a small table close to the window. "Bloody candles! She's obsessed with them." In a fit of pique, he moved the candles on the occasional table, so that they were directly beneath the hems of the curtains. He cackled. "This'll teach the bitch." Neville pulled a cigarette lighter from his pocket…

He left the house not looking back and thinking, *I'll catch her at work. She'll be at the store working with that lard-arse, Mike Roberts. Ha! She always moans about him sneaking up behind her, touching her, and ogling whenever she uses the step ladder in the shop. I reckon she encourages him. The filthy cow!*

Neville had a headache. Apart from the cider he'd just taken from the fridge, he'd not had a proper drink for about 24 hours. If he could just get some cash from Angharad – or maybe from that perv, Mike Roberts, he could stock up on booze, even if it were just a few cans of Tennent's. A gram or two of coke wouldn't go amiss, either – or a bit of grass, perhaps. *Bloody headache. If I drink, I get a headache. If I don't drink, I get a headache. Bollocks!*

Pulling up outside Roberts' Village Store, Neville peered through the window, but could not see his wife. He entered the shop and immediately made eye contact with Mike Roberts who was standing behind the checkout. Mike obviously remembered Neville – and not fondly, either. "Oh, it's you. What do you want?"

"I've come to have a word with my missus. Where is she?"

"Well, she's not here. I haven't seen her for a couple of months now – since she left to work at that farm where your lad Denny works. Tan-y-Bryn isn't it?"

"Oh right." Neville turned to leave. "She couldn't wait to free herself from your wandering hands, I guess." He laughed as he moved towards the door.

"Clear off – and don't come back!"

Neville thought, *it would be fun to smash his face in. He is quite a big blighter, though. Maybe next time.*

He went back to his car and drove off down the valley towards Tan-y-Bryn. As he left the village, he passed a fire engine and a police car heading in the opposite direction, lights flashing and sirens blaring. He giggled and spoke out loud to himself.

"Ooh dear. I wonder where they're off to."

A while later, Neville drove warily into the yard at Tan-y-Bryn. He knew where the farm was, as he'd once dropped Denny off during the summer break a couple of years before. However, he knew nothing about the layout and had no idea where Angharad might be. He didn't know who else might be about either. As he drove past one of the large barns, he spotted some movement through a gap between some partially closed doors.

The lad was bigger than he remembered, and his hair had grown longer – but it was Denny. Neville drew up close to the barn and, as he climbed from his car, he looked around curiously, and cautiously. There was a blue Land Rover, a small Fiat, and a motorbike – which he immediately realised could be Denny's. Then he spotted the rear end of a battered old blue Skoda van, just visible to the side of a nearby shed. *Angharad!* Neville walked slowly to the barn and peered inside, before entering.

"Hi folks." Denny had been looking on as Angharad worked in an enclosure checking over a couple of ewes. They both swung round at the sound of a familiar, although unwelcome, voice. "Well now. Isn't this nice? Just like old times, eh? One big happy family."

Angharad opened the gate to the enclosure and stepped out. "Hello Nev. It's been a while. What do you want?"

"Is that all you've got to say? No 'It's good to see you, Neville. How are you? I trust you're well. We've really missed you.' Some welcome."

Angharad was a few feet away from Neville, and she looked over at Denny, who was moving forward as she said, "I can't speak for your son, but as far as I'm concerned, it's not good to see you. I haven't missed you one bit, although I'm happy to have missed all the violence and aggro that goes with you. You're not welcome, Nev – neither here, nor at home. I've no doubt you're here for something though, apart from exchanging greetings. Like I said – what do you want?"

Neville walked towards Angharad and glanced at Denny, who continued to move closer. "Stay out of this Denny, if you know what's good for you." He turned back to Angharad, thinking, *the bitch thinks she's free of me. She reckons she's in charge – but I'm the boss. Always have been. Cheeky sod.* "You owe me Angharad. We were together for years and I provided for you, and for Sonny Boy here. I don't want to move back in with you, or anything like that." *Chance would be a fine thing –*

given that the place is probably a pile of ash by now. Perhaps that was a bit over the top – but who cares. "No. I just need a few quid to tide me over. Call it a handout. I might even pay you back. Fifty quid should do it for now. What do you say?"

"I don't have any money on me Nev and, if I did, I wouldn't give it to you. After giving us grief – violence and abuse – for years, you just cleared off – apparently to live with some millionairess in Caernarvon, or wherever. Did you spend all of her money? Or did you hit her once too often? As for providing for us – ha! That's a joke. As I recall, we got to the stage when you only ever came home when you ran out of money – especially towards the end."

Neville stepped even closer. "Come on, babe. Don't be like that. Just fifty – for old times' sake."

"You must be joking. I'm not getting into all that again." Angharad drew her mobile phone from her pocket. "I'm calling the police."

Neville took a further step forward, knocked the phone from her hand, and punched Angharad, catching her just below her left eye. "You're not calling anyone, you cow." Angharad squealed and, as her hands came up to her face, she fell back against the enclosure dropping to her knees. She caught a glimpse of Denny closing in on his father. Neville leaned to one side and scooped up a piece of tubing about three feet long. The tube was used to help move sections of the enclosures which sometimes needed to be resized, or moved for cleaning.

Neville had a different purpose in mind for it. He swivelled on the spot and swung the tube viciously, so that it met with Denny's upraised forearm.

Chapter 11

Glyn left the house at about 11 o'clock in order to drive down to the village to pick up a few provisions. As he walked across the yard towards his Land Rover, he noticed an old Ford parked next to the barn. He wondered whether it belonged to a visiting rep or perhaps somebody who had come to see Jason. He looked back at the car, which had a broken wing mirror, scuff marks on the driver's door, and a heavy dent on the offside wing; it occurred to him that no rep that he knew would drive a scruffy motor like that, and Jason's friends tended to be at least moderately well off. He then remembered that Jason had left early, anyway, to visit a client in Liverpool.

      Glyn knew that Angharad and Denny were in the barn. Development of the farm shop was moving forward but had paused for a few days as an inspection of the premises by the Food Standards Agency had been scheduled. In the meantime, Angharad was checking over a small number of ewes with foot problems, while Denny was finishing off the siting of a footbath, which was designed to help control the incidence of foot infections in future. Denny had also been cleaning and repairing some of the hurdles. Such maintenance was vital, in order to ensure optimum flexibility at lambing time. Glyn assumed for a moment that either Angharad or Denny had a visitor. However, just as he placed a hand on the door of the Land Rover, he heard Angharad scream, and then Denny began shouting. An unfamiliar voice then rang out.

"You tart. I spent over a year playing nursemaid to that old bag because of you, you bitch!"

Glyn ran to the shed and as he entered, he saw Angharad on her knees slumped against some hay bales. She held her left hand against the side of her face. Glyn could see, however, that she was grimacing, apparently in pain. Denny shouted, "Stop! You've hurt her." As Glyn tried to make sense of what was happening, things developed quickly. Denny stepped between his mother and the man who had apparently assaulted her. The stranger took a step to his right and lifted a short length of steel pipe and, stepping towards Denny, he swung the pipe viciously. As Denny raised his forearm in defence, the pole made contact, the resulting sound almost like a damp stick being snapped. Denny howled and, clutching his forearm, he fell down close to his mother. As Glyn moved forward, he heard Denny gasp, "Please Dad. Enough!" This was Angharad's estranged husband. Glyn had heard him described as a drunken, drug-addicted thug. Although he'd always been reluctant to condemn others on hearsay, it seemed that the tales, in this case, were true.

As Glyn moved into the barn, Angharad's head turned to look in his direction, and the man swung round to face him, still holding the steel pole. "Who the hell are you?"

Glyn ignored him and spoke directly to Angharad. "Are you okay, love? What's happened to your face?"

"Oh – 'love' is it? I suppose this is your fancy man, Angharad?" Although the man was a few feet away, Glyn could detect the smell of drink, combined with something else – possibly cannabis, even though it was only late morning.

Angharad spoke tearfully. "For Christ sake Nev, you've hurt Denny. He needs an ambulance."

"It serves him right for interfering. He should know better."

Denny leant against a hurdle, tears of pain running down his cheeks. Glyn realised that he had to bring the situation to a close – and quickly, so that Denny could get medical help. It was almost certain that he had a broken forearm.

As Glyn moved forward, Neville raised the steel bar. Rather than hesitating, Glyn jumped forward quickly to close with Neville who bought the pipe down in an arc, far too late. His wrist landed on Glyn's shoulder, and the weight and momentum of the pipe caused it to continue spinning like a cheerleader's baton. It missed Glyn completely, whistling as it flew by, but, as it slipped from Neville's hand, it continued to rotate and hit his own lower leg. He wailed and staggered backwards reaching into his jacket pocket as he did so.

Glyn glanced towards Angharad for a moment and saw her eyes turn towards Neville, her mouth opening wide with alarm. As he swung back to face Neville, Glyn saw he was clutching a knife and moving towards him. Glyn felt a mix of terror and rage. It was an all-or-nothing situation. He had no doubt that a man who could beat his estranged wife and break his son's arm with no apparent sense of remorse, would certainly be prepared to stab a stranger, causing serious injury or even death. With the image of a distressed Angharad in his mind, Glyn closed with Neville again. His tactic worked once, so perhaps it would a second time. It was at that instant that Glyn realised that he really was devoted to Angharad. He could not allow this man to hurt her again.

There was a flurry of movement as Neville and Glyn met each other head on. The knife penetrated deep into Glyn's left arm, its point emerging from his inner triceps. Glyn registered the pain inflicted by the knife at the same instant that Neville suffered the impact of Glyn's headbutt which had been delivered with all the venom he could muster. The muscle fibres in Glyn's arm separated at the same moment that the bone and connective tissues in Neville's upper jaw and nose collapsed.

Glyn stepped back as Neville dropped to the floor, both hands clutching his face. Although Glyn felt a dull pain in his forehead, that discomfort was overwhelmed by the agony that he then felt in his left upper arm.

As Neville had fallen away from him, he'd pulled the knife from Glyn's arm, and then dropped it on the floor as he raised his hands to his face. Glyn placed his hand over the wound in his left arm, wincing as he did so. He moved towards Angharad who nodded in Denny's direction.

"I think Denny's arm's broken – and your arm's a mess. We need to get an ambulance here quickly."

At that point, another voice was heard. It was Carys. "I called the police and I also told them we need an ambulance. It looks as if we need at least two ambulances, though. I'll go and get you some towels and I'll see whether we have any bandages."

Glyn called out to her. "Carys. Whatever you find, just leave it at the door there. Don't come into the shed." Carys looked uneasy, and Glyn added, "We'll cope." Carys nodded, and left.

Angharad looked utterly despondent, but was not seriously injured – although her eye was swollen and looked likely to blacken up. Denny, on the other hand, was cradling his right arm with his left, and shaking visibly, obviously affected by the shock, often associated with fractures. Glyn heard him mutter to his mother.

"I'm okay, Mom. Help Glyn. He needs it."

Not for the first time. Glyn was stunned by Denny's maturity and his selflessness. He watched as Angharad retrieved the towels and a piece of bedsheet material which Carys dropped just inside the barn door. There was nothing that Glyn could do for Denny, apart from offering a few comforting words and assuring him that the ambulance would arrive before long. Neville, meanwhile was mumbling incoherently through broken teeth, his lower face a bloody mess. Angharad glanced at him before moving to Glyn, who was struggling to remove his jacket. With Angharad's help, he managed to ease it off and then Angharad wrapped a piece of the bed sheet gently, but firmly around his arm. Angharad seemed reluctant to meet Glyn's gaze, but he could now see a cut below her eye, presumably the result of a punch. Her eye was watering and the area around it was swollen and already starting to darken.

"There. The bleeding should slow if I wrapped it tightly enough. The blade seems to have gone right through the arm." Angharad's gaze fell to the floor and she spotted the discarded knife. She then looked over at Denny and finally, at Neville. She moved to pick up the knife, her fury evidently rising. However, even though he was in pain and beginning to feel somewhat unsteady himself, Glyn could sense the potential for additional conflict.

"No, Angharad. Don't. Leave it. Please. Things have gone far enough."

Neville had managed to retrieve one of the towels that Angharad dropped onto the floor and he was pressing it gingerly against his face. He looked, fearfully now, at Glyn before looking towards the door as he struggled to get to his feet. Glyn was not about to allow him to leave – even though he'd be delighted to see the back of him.

"Don't even think about it! Sit down and wait for the ambulance – and the police. If I have to pick up that pole, I will do – and I'll brain you with it. Seriously." Neville sat down on one of the bales and looked warily over the folded towel, through which blood was beginning to seep. Glyn was starting to feel dizzy and felt a moment of fear as he considered what might happen if he were to pass out. He knew that seeing two of everything wasn't so much a consequence of being stabbed, but rather the result of headbutting Neville. He'd never headbutted anyone before and he'd been shocked to actually 'hear' a crunch as his forehead made contact with Neville's nose and upper jaw. He took a couple of deep breaths and, fortunately, he was able to hang on for a while longer. After a surprisingly short time, a police car pulled up outside, followed almost immediately by an ambulance.

Glyn and Denny were both taken to hospital in one ambulance, while Neville travelled in another, accompanied by a police officer. The whole process was very well-managed as Neville was kept well away from Glyn – although it seemed unlikely that he presented a threat, given what Glyn had done to him. Carys arrived at the hospital a little later, followed shortly afterwards by Angharad.

Fortunately, the break to Denny's forearm was a clean one and, after having it placed in a plaster cast, Denny was allowed to leave. Glyn was recovering in a side room after spending a while in the operating theatre having several stitches in his upper arm. He managed a weak smile as Carys and Angharad – who was wearing sunglasses – walked in.

"Hi, you two. The doc says that Denny's arm will be fine, and mine should be okay, too, in a couple of weeks. How are you, Angharad?" Angharad lifted her sunglasses for a moment to reveal a nasty-looking black eye. Glyn flinched at the sight. "Bloody hell!"

"I'll cope, Glyn – thanks to you. I'm so sorry you ended up getting hurt though." Angharad paused and looked towards the floor. "Anyway – I've got to get off. I'm going to drive Denny to my sister's place." Glyn wanted to say more, but Angharad seemed keen to leave. "I'll contact you later Glyn. Goodbye."

After Angharad had left the room, Glyn turned to his sister. He had so many questions. "Carys…?"

"Glyn. Listen!" Carys pointed towards the door through which Angharad had just departed. "She's lost her home. She's lost everything."

"Eh? What are you talking about?"

"That husband of hers is the worst kind of animal. He's a piece of shit. A real bastard." Glyn was shocked by the venom in Carys's words. She rarely swore and was never quick to criticise others. "The reason the police turned up so quickly, was because they were chasing him. Yesterday, he beat up his employer, an American woman living in Caernarvon, before ransacking her house and leaving her locked in a cupboard. He stole money, along with the car he was driving. Earlier today, he turned up at Angharad's house, broke in, and set fire to the place before leaving. Apparently one of her neighbours saw him and called the police. The police officer said the house is now a burnt-out shell. The neighbour was able to tell the police where Angharad and Denny worked."

"Whoa. That's awful." Glyn paused for a moment. "Where will they live? I could probably put them up at my place."

"I did say to Angharad that we could find a workaround. However, she phoned her sister in Chester and has arranged to move in with her. I understand that Denny will live there as well, although he might also spend some time at his girlfriend's place."

"Chester? That's miles away. She'll struggle to get to and from the farm – especially in that old banger of hers."

"I know. Angharad is in an odd mood – which is understandable I suppose. I do have some concerns though. Hopefully, she'll contact you later."

At that moment, a surgeon came into the room.

"Mr Edwards. It looks as if you'll be okay to go home in a little while. Your wound was wrapped well, and you do not seem to have lost too much blood. We'll check your blood pressure and, if that is satisfactory, we'll let you go."

Two hours later, Glyn and Carys were back at the farm. Glyn felt exhausted and he went upstairs to lie down. He woke up some time later and could hear Carys in his kitchen, evidently preparing something for him to eat. Before going down, he checked his phone and found a text message from Angharad.

Hello Glyn. I hope you are back home and recovering. I'm so sorry for what has happened and for all the trouble I have brought to you. I'm very grateful to you for sorting Neville out – lord knows what might have happened if you'd not been there. However, I feel so bad about everything and even my son is now incapacitated – at least for the time being. It was wonderful of you to give me a full-time job, but it seems that I simply cause problems for those around me. I realise that my timing is awful – especially with the farm shop nearing completion – but 'm going to leave my job on the farm, rather than causing you any more bother. Hopefully, Denny will be back with you before too long. If you need another farmhand, you might ask Denny for the phone number of Ronny Dennis. He is semi-retired, but still does some work occasionally. Thanks so much for everything. Good luck for the future.
Angharad X.

Glyn's gaze hung for a moment on the X – a symbol for a kiss. Was that a sign of affection? Habit? A simple gesture of friendship? He had no idea. Perhaps he'd never know. Suddenly, Glyn felt very low. Things had been going so well. The business was developing, and he was getting on increasingly well with Angharad. He swore out loud to himself. "Bugger!"

When he'd made his way down to the kitchen, his sister had made him a coffee and was cooking him an omelette on toast. "I hope this will be okay for you, Glyn. Will you manage to eat one-handed?"

"I should be fine thanks. I'll chop the omelette up with my fork and lift and eat the toast separately."

"Good. I thought you'd cope. I'm happy to help out where I can, until you're more able." Carys hesitated. "You've had a tough day. Has Angharad been in touch yet?"

Glyn bought the text up on his phone and slid it across the table to Carys. As she read the message, she frowned. She passed the phone back. "You're not at all happy about this are you?"

"No, I'm not. But if that's the way of it…"

"Give her a few days, Glyn. Then make contact. Her mind must be in utter turmoil at the moment. No home, no possessions, no job – and a load of hassle on the horizon as everything goes through court. That copper said that Neville could get twenty years for everything he's done."

"Ah well. I guess that's one positive."

Glyn phoned Denny the following day and, after some discussion with Carys and Jason, he contacted Ronny Dennis, who was able to start immediately, and proved to be knowledgeable and steady, although far less energetic than

Angharad. Glyn also managed to contact one of Denny's pals who had done some work on the farm a couple of years previously. In addition, Carys continued to undertake light work and Jason also helped when time allowed. Although the situation was less than ideal, the farm would at least continue to function.

Glyn's arm injury was such that he hoped to be able to undertake some basic work tasks within a week or so. However, given the circumstances, he found being incapacitated very frustrating indeed. After spending a couple of days mulling things over, he began to think about Angharad's situation and about her history. Denny had told him a little about Angharad's husband, Neville, but Glyn had been completely thrown by the reality of the situation. Neville, he decided, was simply crazy. A psychopath. It suddenly occurred to him that Angharad had done wonderfully well to raise a son like Denny, especially given the violence that they had both suffered for many years. He felt himself wondering why Angharad had not left Neville, or divorced him, years ago. He realised immediately that his reasoning was foolish. Neville was dangerous, and any attempt by Angharad to terminate their relationship could have proven disastrous.

The more he thought about Angharad, the more he regretted the fact that she was no longer around. He missed her. He knew, too, that his feelings about her were based on much more than her developing professional expertise. He had grown increasingly fond of her and he wanted her back on the farm. More than anything. Glyn tried to imagine how Angharad must be feeling. He opened up his laptop, and typed 'Domestic abuse' into a search engine.

Chapter 12

After leaving the hospital, Angharad headed for her sister Becca's house in Chester. However, in spite of his condition, Denny asked her to take a detour to their house near Llanrwst, in order to see if any of their belongings were salvageable. Sadly, they could see as they approached the end-of-terrace property, that there was simply nothing of any use remaining. As the police had told them, the house was completely gutted. Fortunately, the neighbouring houses had escaped with relatively little damage. Angharad spent a few moments speaking to her next-door neighbour, who had called the police and fire brigade after Neville had left. The woman apologised for not acting quickly enough, and Angharad tried to put her mind at ease.

"Don't worry Lucy. In the circumstances, you did us a huge favour, as the police caught up with Neville, anyway, although – as you can see – he did manage to injure both Denny and me. I'm glad to see that your house is not badly damaged." Angharad and Denny left a short while after. They'd lived at the house for some years, and each had mixed memories.

Angharad drove quite carefully to Chester as her car had begun to smoke quite badly and, by the time they arrived at Angharad's sister's house, the car engine was spluttering.

Angharad turned to Denny and said, "We're not having a very good day, are we Son? The car's packing up now. Grief upon bloody grief!"

Denny could see that his mother was on the verge of tears. "Try to look on the bright side mom. At least dad won't be around for a while."

Even though Angharad's mood was low when she reached Chester, over the following couple of days, it descended to sub-basement level. Her sister's next-door neighbour was a car mechanic, and he agreed to take a look at Angharad's car. He told her that the engine would need a major rebuild at the very least and, ideally, would need to be replaced, at a cost of several hundred pounds. His advice was to scrap the car, as a repair would cost more than its worth. When Angharad contacted the company that insured the contents of her house, she'd assumed that she'd be eligible for a substantial pay-out. However, she was told that, as Neville's name was still on the policy, and he was directly responsible for the fire – and the destruction of the contents, the chances of a pay-out of any description were virtually nil – even though Angharad had paid the premiums since Neville's departure.

Angharad had a little money in the bank, but she needed to buy clothes and other personal items, and she was aware that she'd need to cover any future travel costs. She searched desperately for a job locally and was offered some part-time hours in a supermarket in the edge of the town, to start a few days later. Although the role was for maternity cover, it would, at least provide her with a much needed, although limited, income. She'd be happy simply to be in a position to pay some rent. Even though getting a job, raised her spirits a little, she was already finding life at her sister's place to be somewhat challenging. Becca was incredibly fussy in respect of diet – she made it plain that Angharad's fondness for Italian and Chinese food was not something she agreed with, and she huffed and puffed about any odours that lingered when Angharad brought a takeaway back to the house. Bizarrely, however, Becca's diet seemed to consist of high calorie meals such as stews, suet puddings and meat pies. Her preferences were evidently not driven by a need to eat healthily! When at the house, Angharad tended to spend a lot of time in her bedroom and she also retreated to a room at the front of the house, which Becca described as 'the parlour'. Although Angharad was grateful to her sister for accommodating her, the prospect of spending weeks, months, or even years living with her, was simply terrifying. She knew, too, that Denny, who had a folding bed in his own small box room, also found the environment stifling – so much so that he was cadging lifts or commuting to Betws, where he was spending more and more time at his girlfriend's house, sometimes stopping over.

    After being at her sister's for almost a week, Angharad's state of mind was very low indeed. She'd begun to realise that, of all the things she no longer had access to as a result of Neville's attack, the most significant 'loss' was Glyn. Would she ever see him again? Could she make her way to Tan Y Bryn to see him? Would he welcome her – or was she now simply history, an ex-employee, as far as Glyn was concerned?

On Friday morning, she was sitting in the parlour looking into the front garden, thinking about how a few plants might brighten up the front of the house. She was distracted by movement in the street to her right, and she turned to see two figures approaching the house. It took a moment to recognise them, as each had one arm in a sling.

Her sister answered the door, and Angharad rushed to the mirror over the fireplace and hurriedly tried to shake out her long blonde hair before 'styling' it with her fingertips. She was panicking. *Damn. My hairbrush is upstairs – along with my makeup. Crikey, Angharad, you scruffy, unattractive bugger!*

A minute later, Becca put her head around the door. "Angharad. Glyn is here to see you. Denny and I will be in the kitchen. He wants me to show him how to make apple crumble, apparently." In any other context, Becca's statement would have been bizarre – but Angharad guessed that Denny, that clever and intuitive son of hers, was engineering a one-to-one between her and Glyn.

Glyn walked in, smiled broadly at Angharad, and looked briefly around the room, before approaching her and planting a gentle kiss on her cheek.

"Hi Angharad. How are you feeling? Or is that a silly question?"

Angharad's pulse had risen as soon as she'd seen Glyn approaching the house. She was now feeling quite faint and she placed her hand on the corner of the dining table to steady herself. Glyn could sense that Angharad was a little shaky.

"Are you okay?" He placed his right hand on her arm.

"I'm coping Glyn, thanks." She looked up directly into his eyes and began to shake markedly. Then, the pent-up misery that had been building up inside her since the incident on the farm, burst forth. She began to sob. "Oh Glyn ..."

"Look, Angharad. I know things have been awful for you. In truth, I can't imagine how you're feeling or, come to that, how you're managing to cope." Glyn paused, as he found it difficult to adequately express his concerns. "The thing is, you seemed to be enjoying your job at the farm, and you were getting to be darned good at it. What I mean is, we don't want to lose you."

Angharad looked up at Glyn, her eyes misting up. "Glyn. You don't understand."

"Maybe not. So, tell me Angharad. Make me understand. Please."

"For crying out loud, Glyn. I've lost everything. The house I lived in was burnt to the ground, along with all my possessions, my clothes, furniture that I'd bought over the years. Everything. My sister's been good enough to let me stay here but…" Angharad lowered her voice. "Well, she's a control freak, and she drives me bonkers. Now – to top it all – my motor has packed up, and can't be repaired. No clothes, no car … no money … I'm 36, and I've got nothing left … I'm useless." Glyn reached forward and lifted his left arm carefully and slipped it from its sling, before placing both hands gently on Angharad's shoulders. She looked up directly into his eyes. "I've got nothing. Nothing!" She began to sob, banging both of her fists into Glyn's chest.

♥♥

It would have been easy for Glyn to have told Angharad not to be so silly – but he held back, as he recalled what he'd discovered during his internet search into the subject of domestic abuse. When he did speak, he chose his words carefully.

He said, " Angharad, your ex has gone. It's unlikely that you'll ever see him again – unless it's across a courtroom. I will sort you out a car if you wish – it's no big deal. If you prefer to call it a business motor so you can go out and about to get supplies and meet customers and so on, that's fine. As far as having nothing is concerned – well, it might feel that way, but it's not quite right. You have a roof over your head here – and you also have the option of moving into a hut on the farm." Glyn picked up the look of surprise on Angharad's face. "I'm serious, Angharad. You can move into a hut tomorrow, if you wish." Glyn gave her a moment to assimilate what he was saying, before continuing. "You have a job with a wage, you have a son who thinks the world of you, and you have me."

"What do you mean, I have you?"

"You have me in any way you wish – as your employer and your friend, I hope. And in any other way you want."

"I'm sorry Glyn. I'm not sure what you're saying."

Glyn hesitated "I don't want to exploit the situation by taking advantage of you while you're feeling so low. Maybe we can pick this up a little later – when you're feeling better. Meanwhile – please just let me sort you out a car."

"Okay – but I want you to take money from my wages, to pay for it."

Glyn stepped out into the hallway, feeling almost overwhelmed by an immense sense of relief. He retrieved the bunch of flowers he'd left on the telephone table and, turning round, handed them to Angharad. "These are for you. Get well soon. Please."

She took the flowers. "Thank you, Glyn. They're lovely. Golly – you're telling me to get well soon and all I have is a bruised face. I haven't even asked you about your arm. How is it?"

"The arm's coming along fine. I don't plan on any more punch-ups in the near future, mind." As Angharad looked to the floor, Glyn added, "Sorry love – bad joke." He, turned, and, as he walked from the room, he added, "I'm glad you've reconsidered – and not just because of that Ronny Dennis.

Angharad called after him, "What do you mean?"

"In truth, he is a really nice chap, but … well … let's just say he's a little bit slow off the mark. Ronny the Rocket he isn't!"

As he left the room, he looked back as Angharad lifted her hand to her face to conceal a giggle, along with a few further tears.

"I'll give you some time to think Angharad. I'll call you tomorrow. Oh, by the way – is your phone working? I couldn't get through earlier."

"I'm sorry. I ran out of credit and I switched it off. I know I can still receive calls – but … I don't know really. I'm just being stupid, I guess."

"Will you switch it back on? We'll sort out some credit later." Glyn winked. "Bye."

After calling through to the rear of the house to say goodbye to Denny and to Angharad's sister, Glyn walked back to the station. As he did so, he reflected on what had just happened.

In addition to being understandably depressed, Angharad had been flustered, tripping over her words. She'd been incredibly self-critical 'I'm useless!' and reluctant to believe that all was not lost for her. 'I've got nothing. Nothing!' Glyn had read online that those who have suffered domestic abuse tend to have low self-esteem and may blame themselves for their problems, and even isolate themselves – hoping the problems will simply go away. *I ran out of credit and I switched it off. I know I can still receive calls – but …* He also knew that many sufferers lacked the financial resources to turn things around. There was an irony there, he realised, as Angharad had been developing that financial independence before Neville had turned up and, within a couple of hours, had seemingly taken everything away from her. It was little wonder that she was overwhelmed by feelings of hopelessness. Although Glyn desperately wanted to develop a relationship with Angharad, he realised that, whatever else happened, she'd need time to recover from Neville's nastiness, while building a renewed sense of independence for herself. Glyn was determined to help her in any way he could, but he had no wish to make her feel trapped by his support.

Glyn got off the bus in the village, and walked up the lane towards the farm. As he was walking down the driveway, a message came through onto his phone. It was from Angharad, who was using Denny's mobile.

Hi Glyn. It was lovely to see you today – although, given my mood, you might not have found the visit so wonderful. Anyway, I hope to put some credit on my phone in the next few days. However, my sister says you can phone the landline here if you need to speak to me.

Angharad had provided her sister's number. She signed off with, Angharad X. Glyn slid his phone back into his pocket.

That kiss again. Little things. As he entered his house, Glyn looked around his living room, which he'd furnished with modern, yet comfortable Swedish-designed furniture. He compared it with the room in which he'd spoken with Angharad. It had been years since he'd heard the term 'parlour' used to describe a room in a house. He almost sensed a sneeze building as he inhaled imaginary dust from the dark wooden furniture, china ornaments, and a faded floral sofa. He was certain that neither Denny nor his mother would tolerate living in that environment on a long-term basis.

Chapter 13

That night, at her sister's house in Chester, Angharad slept fitfully, as she kept reliving the day's events in her mind, in particular, Glyn's visit. She hadn't really expected him to travel to Chester, although, she had certainly hoped to see him at some stage in the near future. She'd been giving some serious thought to her decision to leave her job at Tan-y-Bryn, but, given that she now lived so far away and did not have a reliable motor, she'd felt that she had no choice. Maybe. On reflection, perhaps she was simply terrified of Glyn's reaction to the whole episode. After all, it was her presence at the farm that drew Neville there. Then again, was it really all her fault? She would hardly have put Denny, Glyn, or herself in danger deliberately. Should she have anticipated a visit from Neville at some stage? Perhaps. However, surely she could not be expected to spend the rest of her life looking over her shoulder? No! She now had to look forward. As Glyn had said, she had a son who thought the world of her, and she had friends at Tan-y-Bryn. Then there was Glyn, himself. She got the impression that Glyn liked her a lot. Why else would he be so keen to help with the purchase of a new motor and even offer to accommodate her at the farm? Yes – he obviously liked her a great deal. Then again, on reflection, perhaps it was even more than that. What was it he'd said? "You have me in any way you wish – as your employer and your friend, I hope. And in any other way you want." Glyn had been reluctant to expand on that – but those words, "… in any way you wish." If only she wasn't still married to Neville!

And how did she feel about Glyn? She thought for a while, her mind scrolling through a series of memories and images accumulated over the previous few months. She thought about their initial spiky encounter in the barn, and recalled how their relationship had developed from that point. Ultimately, she found Glyn to be honest and fair, helpful, warm and friendly, funny, occasionally a bit grumpy, but generally cheerful – and cheering. He'd also shown himself to be gallant and tough – far too tough for Neville at any rate, which was just as well! So, how did she feel about him? That was easy. She smiled at the thought. She loved him.

The following morning, Glyn decided to give Denny a call, before contacting Angharad. It was just after 11.00, and Glyn was intrigued to learn that the lad was back at his girlfriend's house in Betws. When he remarked on this, Denny was blunt.

"My aunt's a control freak."

Glyn stifled a chuckle as he recalled Angharad using exactly the same phrase. "A control freak? In what way?"

"She has tea at 6.30 and no later, or you have to go out for chips or a takeaway, as she doesn't like you to cook in the kitchen in the evenings. She got the huff when I came home late, and she says that, if my girlfriend visits – which, to be honest, is unlikely to happen – I'll have to sit in the parlour with her, rather than taking her to my room."

Glyn giggled. "Blimey. Church on Sunday?"

"I'd prefer not to be in Chester to find out."

"Yes – I gather that your mother isn't too keen to be there either."

"I think my mum can probably cope but, in truth, I reckon she'd much prefer to be somewhere else, too."

"Listen, Denny. I don't know whether your mum told you about our conversation yesterday – but I offered to sort out a car for her, and I also said that she could move into a hut on the farm."

"Yes. She was really pleased about the car, and said, if it was reliable, she could drive to and from Chester to Tan-y-Bryn. She also mentioned the possibility of the shepherd's hut, but she seemed a little uncertain about it. I get the impression that she doesn't want to make assumptions, although I know she'd be more than happy to move out of her sister's home if possible."

"And what about you, Denny?"

"Oh – it looks as though I'll be staying here for a while. Lisa's parents are really nice people, and said that I can have a room here as long as Lisa is happy for me to stay, and as long as I don't misbehave. I think they trust me though. I told them I'll pay them some rent."

Glyn was reminded at that moment that Denny was not yet 18, although, for his age, he was very mature. It was good to be able to ask him about his mother – although he was careful not to embarrass the lad. Finally, Glyn asked Denny how his arm was and how he was feeling generally.

"The arm is as good as could be expected, I guess. I'll be happy to get this plaster off though. It makes my arm sweat and it itches like mad. As far as how I'm feeling generally goes – well I'm okay, and looking forward to getting back to work. Is that what you mean?"

"Well – yes and no. I realise I should have asked you about this earlier, but my mind has been very much focused on your mom. Obviously, when I speak to her, I'm conscious that she's gone through a traumatic experience at the hands of her husband – and she's lost a hell of a lot. It strikes me, though, that in addition to having a broken arm, with everything that involves, you must also have lost a whole lot. I mean, your possessions at home – clothes and loads of other stuff. Then there's the fact that it's your father who's responsible. I guess it's easy for outsiders, including me, to forget about all that. The whole episode must have hit you very hard, too."

"To be honest, Glyn, losing stuff is more irritating than anything – particularly things like my birth certificate and driving licence – but they can be replaced without too much bother. I've been out and bought a jacket and a pair of jeans, and my mates have been giving me some kit. So, I'm fine, really. I know there is stuff that can't be replaced – but I'm still here and recovering, and I've been more worried about my mum really. I know that you have too, and I think that's great."

As the phone call ended, Denny's closing comment, 'and I think that's great', echoed in Glyn's mind. He felt relieved.

Glyn's arm seemed to be recovering – almost by the hour. He could even grip and lift with his left hand, but was careful not to 'push down 'in a way that would flex the muscles at the back of his upper arm. He felt that he might be able drive an ATV in a few days, even if he had to drive one handed! Nevertheless, he'd be very happy, and relieved, to have Angharad back on the farm. As he rang the landline number at the Chester house, Glyn prayed to himself that she had not changed her mind about returning.

In the event, Angharad's sister was out of the house when Glyn phoned, so Angharad was able to express her thoughts more openly.

"It's been wonderful that my sister has been able to put me up, but, well – if the offer still holds, I think I would like to move into a hut on the farm."

Glyn resisted the temptation to cheer out loud. "Angharad – of course the offer's still holds, and I confess that I'm relieved, as it would be a fair old trip from Chester to Tan Y Bryn every day."

"To be honest, Glyn, I'll be so glad to get away from here. When we were kids, she was always a bossy-boots and we often squabbled. She seems to have worsened over the years though, and it's no wonder she never married. I know it sounds as if I'm being ungrateful, and I do love her – but she's a stereotypical spinster, I'm afraid. Nag, nag, nag!"

Glyn laughed. "Well – that's sisters for you. Don't tell Carys I said that though."

"Huh. I bet Carys has never nagged you. She's brilliant, and I'm sure she doesn't have a nagging bone in her body."

"I'm glad you think she's brilliant, because she'll probably be coming out to Chester to pick you up, as I'm not up to driving yet. I hope that's okay. Can I suggest early on Saturday morning? I'm guessing she'll also want to help you move into the shepherd's hut."

Chapter 14

Carys drove to Chester in Jason's Audi to pick Angharad up. After loading Angharad's meagre possessions into the car, Carys handed her the keys.

"There you go. You might as well get used to it now. Anyway, I'm struggling a bit at the moment." Carys patted her developing bulge. "Triplets, I shouldn't wonder!"

Angharad was stunned and struggled to decide which issue to address first – the car, or Carys's pregnancy.

"Sorry Carys. You've lost me."

"Okay. Firstly, I'm not expecting triplets – it's a girl, and the little blighter's kicking seven bells out of me. Secondly – Jason is about to take delivery of a new car – the day after tomorrow, I believe. We agreed that, if you're okay about it, you should have this. Although the car's in really good condition, it is a few years old now. Jason will take some money out of the farm's budget by way of compensation. As far as I'm aware, we'll be taking some money from your wages to help fund it. However, Glyn suggested that we take just a nominal sum for the time being, given that you're probably not too well off at present. You'll need to speak to him about it, if you want more detail."

"Wow, Carys. A shepherd's hut and a super car. I don't know what to say."

"You don't need to say anything – as we're all really glad to have you back on the farm."

Angharad's mind was turning summersaults. So much was happening, so quickly. And then there was Carys and Jason's baby. She pointed to Carys's abdomen.

"I thought you didn't want to know whether it was a boy or a girl."

"We didn't – but then we started thinking about names, and it just complicates things if you don't know what you're expecting, so, when I went for a scan yesterday, I asked them to tell me."

The women climbed into the car, and Angharad started the engine, grinning from ear to ear. "A little girl, eh. Brilliant. Have you decided on a name?"

"Yes. We had a few ideas written down, but we've opted for Willow. What do you think?

"It sounds absolutely lovely – and I'm sure she'll be lovely too."

Angharad drove the car back to Tan Y Bryn and, after they'd enjoyed a coffee in Carys's kitchen, Carys showed her round a sizeable recently installed hut, which was big enough to house Denny as well, should he ever need somewhere to stay.

Angharad had seen the hut before, but had not been inside. As she looked around, she was surprised at how well-equipped it was. "Gosh, Carys. This place is really impressive. It seems to have almost everything."

"It's not bad, is it. Jason made a lot of suggestions about how we should fit it out. Having lived in the original hut here for several months, he has some good ideas about what works well, and what doesn't." They walked through into the bedroom. "I realise that it's not what you're used to, and I suspect that it will take you a while to get settled in. How do you feel about it?"

Angharad sat down on the edge of the bed and looked around the room. It was brightly decorated and, given that she could smell fresh paint, it had evidently been decorated only recently. In addition to several pictures on the walls, there was a small vase of fresh flowers on the window-sill. "Carys – it's stunning." After her awful experiences of the preceding days, Angharad struggled to keep her emotions in check, and tears began to trickle down her cheeks. Carys sat down beside her, and placed her arm around Angharad's shoulder.

"Take your time getting comfortable here, Angharad. There's no rush. We don't expect you to throw yourself back into your work immediately. Take a few days, and pick things up gradually. You've been through a lot, after all. By the way, with all that's happened, the team have decided to suspend work on the farm shop for the time being. As Denny and Glyn are still recovering from their injuries, and given that the farm has been in the news for all the wrong reasons, we feel it will make sense not to rush things. Also, as my pregnancy nears full term, I'm not going to be as helpful as I'd like. As I said, although it's great to have you back, we don't expect you to launch yourself back into things immediately. Take it steady."

"Thanks Carys." Angharad retrieved a tissue and, as she dabbed her face, she pointed at the vase of flowers.

Carys anticipated her question. "Glyn bought those – along with the pictures on the wall. He seemed sure that you'd like them."

Angharad looked more closely at the images. They were prints of the Norwegian fjords. She remembered telling Glyn that Norway was somewhere that she'd always wanted to visit and that, one day, she intended to go on a fjord cruise.

"He was right about that. They're lovely." She smiled as she thought about the effort and consideration that Jason, Carys – and particularly Glyn – had put into decorating the hut.

Carys stood. "I'll leave you to sort out your bits and pieces, But I'll pop back in a while to see how you're getting on. I'm going to go down to the village store a little later to pick up a few items so, you could either come with me, or else make me a list and I'll pick up whatever you need."

"Carys – you're seven months pregnant. If anyone should be doing the shopping, it should be me."

"Fair enough. We'll go together – and you can lift the bags into the car. If I go into premature labour, you can wheel me into the maternity ward in a shopping trolley!"

Chapter 15

Angharad started working on the farm the day after moving in. She was in the shed beavering away, when she heard Glyn laughing at the door behind her. As she turned towards him, she realised that he was laughing at her.

"Glyn? What's so funny?"

"Sorry Angharad, I couldn't help it. Just as I came in, I glanced up at the turbines on the hill whizzing round. Then, as I saw you, I was struck by the similarity."

"What?"

"Your hair. You've tied it into pigtails. As you were scrubbing away at that water trough, your head was bouncing up and down, and your pigtails were whizzing round like a pair of windmills." Glyn laughed again.

"Oh right. Does my hair look silly like this, then?"

"No. Not at all. It looks really nice. Angharad-like, in fact."

Angharad narrowed her eyes, trying, unsuccessfully, to look sceptical. "Very funny!" She shook her head, experimentally, and realised that her pigtails were, indeed, rotating. She smiled at Glyn. "Seriously, Glyn – thanks for everything you've done for me. The car, the hut – including the rather impressive décor. Everything – and that's not including sorting out Neville."

"It's great that you've started work so soon, although you could have taken some time out to get settled in."

"That's exactly what Carys said to me – but I prefer to get back to work, to take my mind off everything."

"That makes sense, I suppose. And you're okay in here – given your recent experiences?"

"I should be fine, Glyn. Obviously, there are bad memories, but as Neville is likely to be sent to prison for a good few years, there are positives, too."

Angharad had been stunned by the offer of a hut and a car. Even though the hut was available on a short-term basis, the rate she was being charged was little more than a pittance. The same applied to the car. For a moment, she held an image of her old van being loaded onto the back of a scrap lorry. Yes – she was looking forward to using an up-to-date, and almost new-looking Audi estate. It seemed that her life had been 'restarted', and she had the people at Tan Y Bryn to thank for that. Especially Glyn. She did have some concerns about how things would develop in the following months, however.

"Glyn. You know that I'm very grateful for all that you, Carys and Jason have done for me. The thing is, I've been giving some thought to the future, and I'm not sure how soon I'm going to be able to get a place of my own. It could be a few months."

Glyn looked puzzled. "I'm not with you Angharad. What do you mean?"

"Well – the hut is brilliant, but you bought it to let to holidaymakers. Having me in there – especially given the peppercorn rent you're charging me – must be costing you money. You'll need me out as soon as possible, so you can start letting it at a profitable rate."

"Angharad. As you say, we bought the huts for letting, essentially to holidaymakers during the summer season. Originally, we thought we could also make them available to any temporary farmhands working here during lambing. However, you and Denny are working very effectively, and have managed most of the extra work during lambing – and afterwards – yourselves, with very little extra help. Now, if you're desperate to move off the farm, that's fine. However, please take your time. As far as holiday lets are concerned, we've not moved fast enough to capitalise on high season this year and, in truth, we've planned provisionally to have the letting side of the business fully up and running next year, not this. It's likely that the farm shop won't be fully up and running for a good few weeks yet either. These are issues that Carys has put on the agenda for our next company meeting and, hopefully, you'll be able to attend, and perhaps make some suggestions about future development. In the meantime – do try to relax a little. Please." Glyn turned to go. "I'll leave you in peace, but, if you need anything, and I'm not about, just give me a call." He moved towards the door, but hesitated. "Oh – there's one other thing." Angharad waited for him to continue. "I do hope you don't feel threatened by me. I'm not normally violent – but I realise that I must've come across as a psycho when I fought with Neville. The thing is, though, I didn't know how else to handle the situation, and I couldn't bear the thought of you and Denny suffering further. I just had to stop Neville."

    Angharad smiled and then giggled softly as she walked up to him. "Glyn – there's a big difference between being protective – masculine, if you like – as you were, and being an evil maniac, like that husband of mine. I certainly don't feel hostility towards you, or any fear. I'm just so glad that you were on hand. I've thought a lot about what happened, and I can't help wondering what Neville might have done next, if you'd not turned up when you did – especially given Nev's state of mind when he came into the shed." She stepped forward, and placed a kiss on Glyn's cheek. "Thank you, Glyn."

Glyn left the shed, reliving the previous few moments. He could still sense the warmth of Angharad's lips on his cheek. He felt elated. Before returning to the farmhouse, he walked round to the rear of the building to Jason's office. Jason was poring over some documents and Glyn was uncomfortable about disturbing him, so turned to leave. As he did so, Jason tapped on the window and beckoned him inside.

"Hi Glyn. How's it all going?"

"It's all good thanks, Jason. I can see you're busy, so perhaps I should come back later."

"No need. I was about to take a break for a coffee anyway. I'll do you one"

The pair talked for some time about general farm business and about possible next steps in regard to the holiday lets and the farm shop.

Quite suddenly, and to Glyn's surprise, Jason threw in a curve ball. "And what about Angharad?"

"What do mean?"

"Well. First – how is Angharad settling in?"

"I've just been speaking to her. She seems absolutely delighted with all that we've put in place for her – the car, the hut, everything."

"That's good. And second – have you asked her for a date yet?"

Glyn was stunned. "What?"

"Have you asked her for a date?"

Glyn was about to deny even considering such a thing – but he realised that Jason knew him better than that.

"I have to admit that I'd like to, but it would feel wrong – as if I were exploiting her situation. Do you know what I mean?"

"Yes – and I think you're probably right to hold back for a while. A few days at least."

"Do you think so?"

"Yes, I do. Then, when you do ask her, explain your concerns to her. It'll be tricky – but you'll manage."

"Thanks Jason. Good advice as ever."

Chapter 16

Jason and Glyn had left early in Jason's car. They'd driven to Shrewsbury for a two-day conference focusing on all aspects of holiday letting. Denny, meanwhile, was away on an autumn break in Scotland with Lisa. Carys whose pregnancy was approaching full term, was working indoors on admin tasks, and, as a result, Angharad was effectively 'in charge' on the farm.

It was early afternoon as she drove the ATV back down the hill towards the farm. She'd been out on a routine drive around the pastures to make sure that everything was in order. It was mid-October and, to some extent, at that time of year, the sheep looked after themselves, fattening up on relatively lush grass, as the tupping season kicked off in earnest. Nevertheless, it was always wise to keep an eye on things. She recalled a time as a child, when almost half of her father's flock discovered a gap in a hedge and, spying some fresh green growth just a few metres beyond, broke through in order to take advantage of the feast on offer. Unfortunately, the said fresh green growth was situated on the central reservation of a busy dual carriageway that ran past the farm. The resulting chaos, involving the intervention of police, fire brigade and neighbours, had a lasting impact on Angharad's memory and, presumably, on the memories of all those involved. Angharad had learned that, when it came to managing sheep, it made good sense to check, and double check, all aspects.

As she approached the lower gate to the yard, she caught sight of Carys standing just a few feet from her own front door. She sensed immediately that something was not quite right. Carys stood, slightly bowed, with her hands clutching her swollen abdomen. As Angharad drove through the gate, Carys turned and waved. And then she grimaced. Although – ewes aside – Angharad had only limited experience of pregnancy herself, she realised immediately, that Carys was in labour. As Angharad pulled up and switched off the ATV, Carys stepped forward.

"Things started happening earlier this morning with the baby. I began having contractions. I wasn't sure what they were at first – they were like a sort of intermittent dull twinge in my back, and I thought it was too early anyway, as I'm not due for a couple of weeks. They've become stronger and more regular though – every few minutes now. I think I need to get to the hospital fairly quickly. I've tried phoning Jason, but there's no answer, so I left a message.

Angharad climbed from the ATV, and placed her hand on Carys's shoulder. "Okay Carys. You can try calling Jason again in a while, and I'll try to get in touch with Glyn. I'm sure you know more about conferences than I do, but I'm guessing they have their phones switched to silent during presentations. I'm sure we'll make contact before long. In the meantime, I suggest we get you ready to travel because, the way you describe it, you've probably been in labour for a good few hours now."

Carys had prepared for the hospital visit and had a bag packed. It took Angharad just a few minutes to swap her boots and jacket for tidy trainers and a sweatshirt – and the two women were soon heading towards the hospital in Angharad's car. As they drove, Carys's contractions became more frequent and Angharad began to keep a mental 'tally'. By the time they were just a few miles from the maternity unit, the interval between individual contractions was less than five minutes, and Carys was beginning to breathe more deeply each time her body tensed. Angharad could sense that Carys was becoming stressed and she tried to lighten the mood a little.

"You're lucky we're travelling in the Audi, Carys – rather than my old van. If I were still driving that, you could expect to give birth in a lay-by on the Holyhead Road – and I'm not sure how that would look on the birth certificate."

Carys responded with cross between a grin and a grimace, as another contraction kicked in. "Thanks for those few words of comfort, Angharad."

"Sorry Carys. I'm just trying to distract you, to help make the pain less of an issue." She smirked, and added, "Maybe my ploy's not working."

"Maybe."

"Anyway – you're out of sync."

"Eh?"

"The baby's way too early. Lambing starts in March. Trust me. I know about these things."

"Angharad?"

"Yes, Carys?"

"Stop it!"

"Yes boss." Both women laughed. Angharad's ploy, it seemed, was working, after all.

As they were driving into Bangor, Jason phoned to say that he and Glyn were on their way back from Shrewsbury. He planned to drop Glyn off at the farm on his way to the hospital.

It was approaching teatime on the following day when Jason, Carys, and their baby daughter returned to the farm. After they'd had a chance to settle in at home, Glyn phoned Angharad and asked her if she'd care to accompany him, as he was about to go around next door to check on the couple and the new arrival. Angharad was delighted to do so.

"That would be nice. Although I took Carys to the hospital, I left when Jason arrived, and I've yet to meet little Willow in person."

"I've not seen her either." Glyn hesitated. "Blimey. I've just realised – I'm an uncle!" Angharad sniggered.

Jason ushered them into the lounge where Carys had just fed Willow. Glyn remarked that the baby was both pretty and peaceful.

Jason nodded. "Yes – she's lovely isn't she, and she's certainly peaceful. I've yet to hear her cry."

Angharad said, "Hah! Be careful what you wish for Jason. I remember that, after Denny was born, he was so quiet, for so long, that I worried that there was something wrong with him. Anyway, after a few hours, he discovered his lungs. And he made full use of them. He made so much noise, I was worried that…well…you get the idea." At that moment, Willow began to gurgle. "There you go. She's thinking about it."

Carys handed the baby to Angharad, laughing, "She's all yours, Angharad. If she cries now, we can blame you." Angharad beamed as she gently rocked the child. Carys then added, "We've decided to call the baby Willow, Cristyn, Angharad, Garrington – Cristyn being my late gran's name and Angharad…well…Jason and I thought Angharad is quite a pretty name – and we do know someone with that particular handle…"

After a minute or so, Angharad passed Willow to her 'Uncle Glyn'.

Chapter 17

On a few occasions, Glyn had been away overnight on business. He'd been to a couple of conferences, including an event in Chepstow focusing on all aspects of diversification in farming and, of course, he'd also been to one with Jason. Although it was sometimes a relief to get away from the farm – as the business could be intense at times – Glyn was beginning to enjoy being away from home less and less. When they'd learned that Carys had gone into labour, Jason and he had left the Shrewsbury conference immediately. As they drove back, Glyn felt some relief that they would not be stopping over at the hotel conference venue. When he considered his reasons for this, he realised that, in addition to being concerned for his sister, he was also missing Angharad. He began to wonder what it was about Angharad that he found so appealing. She was hard-working, reliable, well organised, intelligent and considerate. But that wasn't it! She was fun to be around. She was pretty, and she was shapely. He loved her sometimes wild wavy blond hair and her bright smile. She was attractive – but in a 'girl-next-door' sort of way. When she was not working, she often wore fairly tight jeans, and, once, when he called round to her hut, she answered the door wearing patterned yoga pants. She tended to sway a little when she walked. Glyn couldn't help thinking that she was actually rather sexy!

Over the following few weeks, Glyn and Angharad worked together on the farm fairly frequently. Glyn sometimes accompanied Angharad as she moved around the meadows distributing extra feed, to help compensate for the fact that, as the weather cooled, the grass grew more slowly. Angharad helped Glyn with maintenance tasks around the yard, and she even found herself on the roof of the lambing shed on one occasion. However, Glyn seemed uncomfortable with what he called a potentially risky activity for a '30-odd' year old woman. Angharad's response was, perhaps, predictable. She narrowed her eyes and said, "Oh right! Risky for an old woman, eh? Sexist and ageist. Huh! Anyway – you're older than me…Grandad!"

"Angharad – behave yourself. Anyway – I didn't say you were an old woman. I said you were a 30-odd year old. You do seem to be in pretty good nick, though, for a mature woman."

Angharad, who, at that moment was standing 20 feet up on the edge of the roof, said, "In pretty good nick, eh? I suppose I should take that as a compliment. Of sorts." She smiled and, not for the first time, Glyn felt a ripple of excitement as he sensed their relationship progressing.

Later, Glyn invited Angharad to join him for mid-morning coffee and toast in his kitchen. It was just a couple of weeks before Christmas, and, after enjoying elevenses and a cosy chat, Angharad asked him whether he might wish to visit her for Christmas dinner. Glyn said, "Ordinarily, I'd love to. However, I understand that Carys and Glyn will be inviting both of us round to theirs. I haven't said anything before, as I didn't want to pre-emp anything, but Carys confirmed last night. I guess she'll tell you what's happening when she sees you."

Jason and Carys organised a Christmas lunch at their house, and, as Glyn predicted, they invited him and Angharad. Although Carys and Angharad took care of the cooking, Jason and Glyn volunteered beforehand to take care of the washing up afterwards. Much to the amusement of the Tan Y Bryn women, Glyn announced that he and Jason had discussed the issue in some depth and they'd elected to act like 21st Century men, by picking up some of the work usually associated with women. The announcement met with something of a withering look from Carys, whilst Angharad said, "Wow! 21st Century men, eh? So, that's a bit different to 20th Century men, I suppose?" Both men nodded in agreement. "Well – how would it be, if Carys and I acted like 21st century women?" The men nodded again, although a little hesitantly, this time. Angharad turned to Carys. "Shall we go down to the village inn and leave them to sort out the dinner?"

Jason interrupted. "The pub's closed. It's Christmas day, remember."

Turning to Angharad, Carys said, "Bugger! Ah well. It was worth a try, I suppose. Maybe next year."

The relaxed and playful mood continued throughout the afternoon, and Angharad felt a growing 'closeness' to Glyn, as they chatted and joked, and exchanged smiles. Indeed, Angharad was almost sorry to leave in the late afternoon, as she had to prepare tea in her hut for Denny and Lisa who were due to visit her. She said goodbye to Jason and Carys, and Glyn accompanied her to the door. As they stood in the hallway, she looked up into Glyn's eyes. "Thanks Glyn. It's been a really nice day – one of the best Christmases ever."

"I've enjoyed it too – although I guess it's all down to Carys and Jason – and you as well, as you did much of the cooking."

"Nevertheless, Glyn."

"Yes?"

"Thank you." Angharad gave Glyn a brief kiss on the lips, before turning to leave. She'd have liked to have invited Glyn to tea, but felt that her hut was a little too small to accommodate four.

Glyn returned to the living room, grinning and, much to his surprise, it was Carys who said, "You two certainly seemed to be enjoying each other's company today. Is there anything we need to know about?"

"What do you mean?"

"Do you have any dates planned?"

Glyn looked at Jason. "Jason – is this your doing?"

Jason shook his head. "No way. You can see Carys's point though. We can both see how close you two are becoming – and you were going to ask Angharad out weeks ago."

"I know – but I'm struggling to figure out how best to go about it. I'll ask her soon. I promise."

Chapter 18

As the year approached its end, Glyn was pleased with how things were progressing, but he was still unsure about how best to ask Angharad to go out on a date with him. Inspiration came from an unlikely source.

It was early on Monday morning, and Glyn was in the village collecting a few groceries. The day was particularly windy, and, as he came out of the village store, a newspaper rack just outside the door blew over, casting its contents to the elements. Glyn scurried about gathering up the newspapers and magazines, before carrying them back into the shop – and placing them on the counter, to the delight of the shop assistant. He climbed back into his Land Rover, and dropped his bag onto the passenger seat. As he turned to face the road, a sheet of newspaper – one that he'd evidently missed – flew up onto the windscreen directly in front of him. Glyn wound down the side window and reached out to retrieve it, and, as he did so, he noticed an advert promoting a special event at a cinema in the nearby town of Rhyl. He read the advert in detail, before sending a text to Angharad.

Hi Angharad. They sometimes have special film nights at the cinema in Rhyl, featuring older films. In a couple of weeks' time, they're having a post-Christmas event where they're NOT showing any Christmas-themed films (Apparently, they're offering an alternative to all the mushy Xmassy stuff that we've been overwhelmed with on the television of late!). Instead, they're showing something called Mr and Mrs Smith, featuring Brad Pitt (almost as good looking as me) and Angelina Jolie (almost as good looking as you). I missed it first time round. It is a bit violent though. Alternatively – next week, they're showing something called Finding Your Feet. It's about oldies coping with life's changes (ouch!). Two questions: a) Have you seen either of them? b) Can I treat you to a bag of post-Christmas popcorn? Glyn.

He checked back through the message and was about to hit the send button, when he decided to add an X. He glanced again at the final line: *Can I treat you to a bag of post-Christmas popcorn? Glyn. X.* He hit send before he had chance to change his mind.

A short time later, Angharad responded.

Hi Glyn. A friend of mine has seen the 'oldies' film and she says it was great, so: a) No, I haven't seen it. b) Post-Christmas popcorn sounds good.

By the way – you're as cranky as a kettle full of wasps. But, thankfully, a lot friendlier.

PS I'm looking forward to the film. Angharad XX

Glyn was delighted with the response. *As cranky as a kettleful of wasps* – and two kisses!

Later that evening, Glyn sent another message.

Hi Angharad. Yes, it's me again. I just wanted to apologise, really, for not asking you out on a date before now. I suspect that we're both aware of the potential tensions in an employer-employee relationship when things become personal. It was tricky when I was just your employer, but now, I'm your landlord as well! I guess it's for those reasons that I've not asked you for a date before. I admit that I've wanted to ask for a long time, but felt that it would be unfair to you. I was afraid that you might feel obliged to say yes – that you could feel intimidated as I was your boss. More recently, though, I began to feel that my attitude was quite patronising really, as I know you're quite able to speak your mind. Beyond that, I've struggled to find the words to ask you for a date. Perhaps I just lack confidence. Maybe I'm simply a bit slow. XX

Glyn's text did not include any questions, so there was no requirement for Angharad to answer. However, Glyn waited patiently, hoping she'd respond. She did.

Hi Glyn. After my relationship with Neville, it's unlikely that I'd allow myself to be intimidated by any man again, so don't worry about that. I have to admit that, although I have always liked you – even when I said you were hard-nosed, I felt uneasy about 'taking the lead' in respect of forming any personal relationship with you. Also, I didn't want to put Denny in an awkward position, although I now know that Denny is happy for the two of us to become closer. Finally – there's no pressure. If things work out, that's great. If not, so be it – though, hopefully, we'll still be friends.

Oh – as for being slow. Well, I have an image in mind of a wheelbarrow full of tortoises – and the barrow has a flat tyre! Nevertheless, I'm still looking forward to the film.

XX

Glyn read through her text a couple of times and laughed at her tortoise jibe. *Ha! Cheeky devil!*

Chapter 19

The following day, Denny went into the lambing shed where Angharad was busy repairing a couple of sheep deck chairs.

"Hi Mom. I just bumped into Glyn outside. He seems very cheerful."

"I've no idea why – unless it's because I've agreed to go out with him to the pictures next week."

"Wow – a proper date?" Angharad nodded vigorously, and Denny added, "About time too."

"Yes. I'm looking forward to it, although I do feel a bit guilty."

"Guilty? About what?"

Angharad looked towards the shed door and, lowering her voice, she said, "Denny – I'm still married."

"Well Glyn knows that – so it's obviously not worrying him too much. I'm sure he realises that you're not about to take Dad back into your life – if he ever gets out of prison."

"That's not what I mean. I feel that I'm carrying baggage. I guess, I'm looking for a clean start. Do you understand? I'm really proud of you, and what you've achieved, but, as far as my relationships are concerned, I want to be able to do my own thing, freely, without your dad's shadow hovering over me. Perhaps, I expect too much."

Denny thought for a moment. "You should be able to get a divorce from Dad. I mean – he can hardly pretend to be your husband from behind bars, especially given that he left you to live with that American woman. Then there's everything that he's put you through."

"Denny, I'd love to divorce him – just to be able to put him in the background, and to give us both a sense of closure, I suppose. The problem is, knowing Neville, he'll resist a divorce, every step of the way. He'll drag it out, just to exercise every last bit of control."

As Denny left to travel back to Betws, he gave some further thought to his mother's predicament and, by the time he reached his girlfriend's house, he'd made up his mind to visit his father in prison in Wrexham.

The following day, Denny told Carys of his intention and asked for a few hours off work. He didn't go into great detail, but simply said that he was trying to ease the path towards a divorce for his mother. He asked Carys not to mention it to Angharad, until he'd had a chance to feed back to his mother following his visit.

On the following Friday afternoon, Denny rode to Berwyn Prison in Wrexham. He'd never been in a prison before, and felt nervous. However, getting in was straightforward, the prison staff were friendly, and, by the time he sat down face-to-face with his father, any remaining nervousness was displaced by a mixture of anger and disgust at the figure before him. He struggled to keep his feelings in check, as Neville opened the conversation in his usual smug manner.

"Hi Denny. You couldn't wait to see your old dad in nick, eh? Worrying about me, are you? No need. I'm coping. I see your arm's better now. I guess you're back at work on that farm, and earning a few bob. I'm sorry if I put the skids under you for a few weeks. Your mom's not here with you, then?"

"No. She decided to give it a miss. She has no interest in seeing you – you're history. She does want a divorce though, which is why I'm here."

"Oh right. So, you're representing her, are you? Training to be a solicitor, eh?" Neville leant back in his chair and smiled coldly.

Denny simply grinned back at him. "Your cocky attitude is laughable. You might want to listen to what I'm about to say." Neville's smile disappeared as Denny continued. "Before long, we'll be facing each other across a courtroom and I for one will elaborate on the way you've treated Mom and me over the years. I'm going to paint a really black picture to ensure that you get the maximum sentence possible. I'm guessing that Mom will do the same. We both want you out of our lives – Mom especially."

"Listen Son, if you go easy with the evidence and can persuade your mom to do the same, I'll be happy to give her a divorce. I know I'll be in here for a while at least, so she'll be of no use to me."

Denny laughed. "Here we go. Even while in prison, you're trying to control us. But that's all over. Neither Mom nor I will make light of what you've done, but we won't deliberately make things worse for you – as long as you're prepared to give Mom a quickie divorce. If you refuse to do this, not only will I go into great detail about your past behaviour, but I'll also make sure that as many people as possible get to hear all of the grisly details. I'm talking about the press, social media and whatever." Denny bared his teeth, almost snarling at this point. "I'll also make sure that your fellow prisoners get to know what an evil wife-beating maggot you are. I bet they love wife beaters in here."

Denny's words hit home and he could almost sense his father shrinking before him. Having seized the initiative, Denny carried on. "You probably think that I'm afraid of you. That's not the case. The only reason that you got the better of me in the lambing shed, was because I never dreamt that you'd hit me with an iron bar. You're supposed to be my father, for crying out loud. I should say, you *were* supposed to be my father. No, I'm not afraid of you. I simply detest you and I have no wish to be associated with you ever again. You are a sad, drugged up, drunken, psychopathic loser. Goodbye Dad – and a happy New Year!" Denny stood to leave and, as he turned, Neville called after him.

"Okay Denny. You win. You can tell your mother that she can have her quickie divorce. Just don't go over the top with your evidence. You've no idea what some of the people in here are like."

Denny turned back towards his father who, bizarrely, perhaps, seemed to be shaking – presumably with fear. Reality bites! thought Denny. He nodded, and, as he left the room, he smiled. *Job done!*

After leaving the prison, Denny went directly back to the farm. His mother had finished work for the day and was preparing some food in her hut. She was happy to see him.

"Hi Denny. This is a surprise. I thought you'd be back at Lisa's by now."

"No. I had a few hours out this afternoon. I've only just got back."

"Ah. I wondered why I'd not seen you about, but then you sometimes work in the office on Fridays. Can I ask where you've been?"

"Sure. I've been in prison."

Angharad looked up wide-eyed. "What?"

"No. I haven't committed a crime – though I was tempted. I went to see Dad."

"Now that's a surprise. Whatever for? I can't imagine you're missing his warm smile or his fatherly ways." Angharad hesitated and held her hand up to delay Denny's response. "I'm sorry Denny. That's not fair. If you want to see him, it's not for me to condemn you."

"Mom! If you really believe I wanted to see him … well … you've lost the plot. I'd prefer never to see him again. No – I went to see him on your behalf."

"What do you mean?"

"Well, to cut a long story short, I've persuaded him to let you have a quickie divorce."

Angharad stood with her mouth open, speechless, as Denny began explaining in detail how his visit to the prison unfolded. He finished by saying, "I hope you're okay with what I've done. I decided to do it, as it hurts me to see you so concerned about the future. I felt that things needed tidying up."

Angharad threw her arms around her son. "Denny – you're a bloody marvel. Thank you so much." Angharad was cooking a seafood pasta and offered to do some extra for Denny. After a while, she placed the food on the table and sat down.

"It occurs to me that it would be a good idea to get things moving as soon as possible. I'll phone round a few solicitors, to get a sense of how much this is going to cost. It would be handy to get things underway before Neville goes to court. That could be a while yet, but I'd prefer to act quickly. Also, it's likely to be costly, so I may need a loan from the bank. There's a lot to take care of."

"That makes sense, mom. I might be able to help you out, if necessary. I've got a bit of money saved."

"I'll sort it, Denny, but thanks anyway." Denny was quiet for a moment and Angharad could see that he was uneasy about something. "Are you okay Son?"

"Yes – fine really. I'm just curious, I guess. I can't help wondering why Dad is the way he is. I mean, I don't recall you ever being nasty to him – so why is he such a vile piece of work?"

"That, Denny, is quite a question. You may know some of this – but Neville never knew who his father was – and it's questionable whether his mother, your gran, did either. She couldn't cope with Nev and he ended up in an orphanage run by a religious order and, apparently, he was abused on a daily basis, receiving beatings from nuns and occasional sexual abuse from one of the older boys. I suppose we should feel sorry for him really."

Denny replied, "Maybe – but given his background, you'd expect him to be an altogether different person – just the opposite of what he is. I mean, he had all that suffering piled on him, so you'd never expect him to inflict the same sort of thing on those around him, especially his family. Anyway, how do you know all this?"

Angharad said that once, when Neville was particularly drunk, he told her something about what he had suffered in the home. "I had hoped that sharing the tale might help in some way to 'purge' him of the nastiness within. However – if anything – it made him worse. When he'd sobered up a little, he waved a kitchen knife at me, and told me that he'd cut my tongue out, if I ever revealed what he'd said. I remember being close to wetting myself – it was terrifying. So, Denny – if you ever see your dad again, please, please, please – keep that information to yourself."

"I will do mom. Something else has been playing on my mind."

"Oh yes. What's that?"

I remember, not long before he disappeared, Dad bought a load of drink home. There were a few cans, a bottle of Jack Daniels, and even some gin. I was only 15 at the time, and he seemed determined that I should try all of it. He even offered me a joint."

Angharad shook her head, scowling. "I remember."

"The thing is – he was hardly the most 'giving' of fathers. I mean – generous to a fault, he was not. I couldn't quite figure out what was going on. I had tried beer before, at my mate's birthday party – but I was not all that keen on it and, if anything, I preferred soft drinks. Maybe I was just too young for that stuff, and I still don't like whiskey, now." Denny hesitated, as if reviewing the episode. "I recall you going berserk when you walked in and realised what was happening."

"Yes. I remember. I screamed at him, and he punched me in the stomach. Very nasty. I suppose that I shouldn't really have been so shocked by it all – especially given his previous behaviours. I'm guessing that he'd come into some money – I don't know whether he'd earned it, or stolen it – and he'd decided to share what he'd bought with his 15-year-old son. I suppose I should be grateful that was the only time he tried to get you to follow in his footsteps. I remember speaking to an old schoolfriend whose sister had become a counsellor, specialising in supporting people with drink and drugs problems. She said that it was all too easy for the children involved to imitate the behaviours of alcoholic parents – as that's the life they'd grown up with. I decided that I'd do anything to prevent you from going down that route."

"So that's why you still discourage me from drinking."

"Denny, you're approaching the age when you'll decide for yourself. However, whenever you find yourself starting to wobble, after drinking a bellyful, give some thought to your father. Perhaps, in some ways, his example – although a bad one – could even be of benefit."

"I understand what you're saying Mom – and I'm grateful to you for protecting me. I hope that I'll never let you down."

As the conversation ended, Angharad became a little wistful. As she reflected on a range of interactions with Neville over the years, she was reminded of a pattern of behaviours. Whenever Nev wanted something, he would begin, pleasantly enough, by attempting to ingratiate himself, for example, as he did with Angharad when he first entered the lambing shed. Then, if he was unsuccessful, he'd resort to violence. After Neville had attempted to ply Denny with alcohol, Angharad's response had been robust, and Nev realised that there was no way he could reason with her. As a result, he simply resorted to his default 'fall back', and he hit her – hard!

A little later, as Denny rode off the farm, he spotted Glyn in the yard, hosing down his particularly muddy Land Rover. He exchanged waves, and smiled as he left the yard, to return to Betws, and to his girlfriend, Lisa.

Chapter 20

Angharad and Glyn went to the cinema in Angharad's estate car. They agreed that the Audi would be more comfortable, and easier to park than Glyn's Land Rover. On the way, Angharad told Glyn about Denny's visit to see his father in prison. She didn't go into great detail, but finished by saying that she was incredibly proud of her son. Glyn was also impressed with Denny's efforts.

"That son of yours is an absolute ace. I'm surprised you didn't have any more kids."

"I had Denny when I was 16. The birth was a tricky one, and I had to have an emergency caesarean section. Sadly, even that went a bit pear-shaped, and I was left with some damage to my womb. Later, I was advised to have a hysterectomy – for medical reasons – as having another child was considered to be potentially risky. I was reluctant, and Neville wasn't too keen either. However, the doctors were pretty insistent, so I had the womb removed. No more kids, I'm afraid."

They arrived in time for the early evening viewing, allowing enough time to go for a meal afterwards. They sat in the auditorium for about thirty minutes, watching a seemingly interminable series of adverts before the main event was due to begin. However, as soon as they were seated, Glyn began shuffling in his seat. He was obviously not comfortable, so Angharad asked him if he was okay.

"I'm sorry, Angharad. I've got stomach ache. I've had it on and off for a couple of days now – but I didn't want to threaten our date by making a big deal out of it. I've had something similar before. They said it was probably a rumbling appendix, but it cleared with some antibiotics. I should be fine, but I might decide to pass on the meal. I hope you don't mind."

"That's no problem Glyn. If you don't feel up to this, we can always leave now and reschedule."

"No. I should cope – although I'll probably pop out to see the doctor tomorrow."

As the film started, Glyn seemed to settle and the couple soon became engrossed in the action. However, partway through the film, Glyn again began to writhe in his seat, before excusing himself as he needed to use the toilet.

Angharad waited patiently for him to return, distracted to some extent by the film, which she was enjoying very much. However, after 10 minutes or so, she began to feel a little uneasy. Eventually, after waiting for about 15 minutes, Angharad left the auditorium in order to find Glyn. She spoke to a member of staff in the reception, asking him if he could go into the men's toilet in order to see if her friend was there.

"Aah! I'm sorry to say this but I believe the person you are looking for has just been taken off to hospital in Bangor. He collapsed here in the foyer, obviously struggling with severe stomach pains, so we called for an ambulance. We couldn't get much sense out of him and we had no idea whether he was here alone or with somebody else, although a woman who seemed to recognise him said that she knows his girlfriend who lives in Betws. The paramedics seemed to think that he may well have had a ruptured appendix, so the call was treated as an emergency."

Angharad was astonished that the cinema had not put out an announcement over the public address system. However, her irritation was displaced by her fears for Glyn. Was it really something to do with that stomach ache – the rumbling appendix? Or had he had a heart attack? A stroke? Angharad was frightened and decided to drive straight to the hospital. However, she first rang Carys, who said that she, too, would set off for the hospital straight away. As she drove to Bangor, Angharad wondered briefly about the reference to Glyn's so-called 'girlfriend in Betws', but she dismissed it, assuming that it was a case of mistaken identity.

When Angharad arrived at the hospital, she was told that Glyn had been taken directly to the operating theatre. She spent a nail-biting half hour in the waiting room before being joined by Carys. A short while later, Glyn was wheeled from the operating theatre to the recovery room, but was not yet conscious. After a further half hour, he was moved to a side ward, and Angharad and Carys were able to speak to the surgeon, before going in to see Glyn.

The surgeon described what appeared to have happened. "I suspect he's been experiencing some discomfort for quite a while as an extensive area around the appendix was quite severely infected, causing it to rupture this evening. We removed the appendix and, hopefully, he'll recover well. However, he will be limited in terms of what he can do for a few weeks. Long-term, he should be fine – but he really does need to attend a little more promptly to any aches and pains that he experiences in future."

The two women were allowed to go into the room but, aside from a rather wan smile, Glyn, who was now connected to a drip and a monitor, was not at all communicative and, in fact, was barely awake. Carys and Angharad left after a few minutes, promising to return the next day.

After a restless night, Angharad was up early, busying herself about the lambing shed. She felt that working would help take her mind off Glyn's misfortune. She consoled herself with the fact that it wasn't a heart attack or a stroke and that he should recover fully.

She drove to Bangor to visit Glyn in the early afternoon. Glyn had been moved from the side ward into a larger unit and Angharad had to ask at the ward reception where Glyn was. As she turned to enter the ward, she was stopped by a woman who was just about to leave. She'd obviously heard Angharad asking about Glyn. What happened then both shocked and saddened

Angharad. The woman told her that she just been in to see Glyn.

"I'm Pattie, Glyn's fiancée. I've not seen him for a few weeks, and was really shocked to hear he was so unwell. Anyway, it looks as if he'll be stopping at my place when he gets out of here. Just for a while – until he recuperates. He's a lot better now than he was yesterday. Anyway, I must dash. My taxi's waiting. Bye."

Angharad was gobsmacked, and stood mutely, as Pattie marched off. After a few seconds, she also left. In these changed circumstances, she couldn't bear to face Glyn. She'd heard about Pattie – but understood than Glyn no longer had anything to do with her. If Pattie was back in the frame – assuming that she'd actually ever been 'out of the frame', then maybe, she'd move back to her sister's in Chester. A short while ago, life was looking so much brighter. There was a real future. But, now … for the first time, since she'd first met him several months before, Angharad felt angry at Glyn. Very angry. Her concern for Glyn turned to disgust. Her love turned to disappointment.

Angharad returned to the farm and spent the rest of the day in her hut. She was in an awfully low mood. She switched off her phone in a simple attempt to isolate herself from the outside world, and especially from Glyn. She simply could not fathom his mindset. *How on earth could he do this to me?* She lay in bed considering the future. She'd enjoyed her time in the hut and hated the thought of returning to her sister's in Chester. However, what else could she do?

The following morning, having slept only fitfully, Angharad rose much later than usual and was preparing some breakfast when there was a knock on the door. She assumed it would be either Carys or Denny checking up on her, so she was astonished to see the woman who claimed to be Glyn's fiancée standing there.

"Hi. It's me again. Pattie. Can I have a word?" Angharad was uneasy, slow to respond, and looked at Pattie suspiciously. Pattie was persistent. "Please – I want to apologise." A little reluctantly, Angharad stepped aside and invited her in.

"How did you know where to find me?"

"I've just spoken to Carys. She told me where you were." Pattie hesitated, and Angharad could see that she was becoming tearful. "I'm so sorry. What I did yesterday was awful. Unforgivable. It's true that I used to go out with Glyn – and we were engaged at one stage. However, we broke it off months ago. I loved him – and I think he loved me, but we just weren't compatible. I did not want to live on the farm and he didn't want to live above the cafe. I'm a bit of a homely person – whereas, Glyn likes to 'do' stuff. As I'm sure you know, as a farmer he's really an outdoorsy sort of person. A bit of an action man, in his own way."

"So, why did you tell me you were together."

"Oh – desperation, I suppose. I confess that I've been fairly lonely of late, and so anxious for the attention of a man. A friend of mine was at the cinema and she saw Glyn there. When she told me that he'd collapsed and had been rushed to hospital, all the old feelings for him came back, and I just had to visit him. I told him that I still care for him and that, if he were prepared to give it another go, I'd consider moving to the farm to live with him. I was desperate – and so foolish."

"Well – what did Glyn say?"

"As always, he was very kind. I know he didn't want to hurt me – but he repeated that we're simply not meant to be together, as our needs and our hopes are so different. He said that, although he still cares for me, it could never work for us. I then asked him if he'd met someone else and he said that he had indeed, and that he had high hopes in that regard. Finally, he told me that I was an attractive woman and that there was certainly a man out there for me, somewhere. On reflection, he really was considerate and gentle, but I felt rejected and utterly dejected. I'm so sorry, but, when I heard you talking to the nurse, I knew that you were the one. What I did was simply spiteful. As I climbed into my taxi outside the hospital, I saw you leave and I could see that you were upset. It was all so wrong of me. I'm not normally a nasty person – but I simply wasn't thinking straight. Please don't let what I've done drive a wedge between you and Glyn. He deserves the best."

Pattie's tears were now flowing freely, and Angharad was stunned. For the moment, at least, she was lost for words. She could easily have been furiously angry with Pattie but, somehow, she could identify with the woman's desperation. She stepped forward and placed her hands gently on her shoulders. "Pattie. What you did was certainly unpleasant – but, in a way, I can understand why you did it. In fairness, you've been brave and decent in coming here to see me, so thank you for that. Hopefully, as Glyn suggests, there is a man out there for you somewhere. Good luck."

After Pattie left, Angharad returned to her breakfast, and switched on her phone.

Chapter 21

Glyn's recall of events leading up to his emergency admission was, to say the least, vague. *Okay – I was at the cinema in Rhyl with Angharad. But what happened next?* He'd a foggy recollection of being moved into an ambulance and he remembered that his stomach had been on fire. Absolute agony! Then what? Carys and Angharad had been at the hospital. He couldn't focus. He struggled to stay awake. Fortunately, things were much clearer now. The nurse had been in to check on him. She told him a little about the operation saying that he'd had his appendix removed. However, the doctor would be in later to speak to him in detail about the operation and about what would happen in the near future.

Visiting time's approaching. Hopefully, Angharad will come to see me. Angharad. She's lovely. He hoped there was a future for him with Angharad.

Glyn was stunned when Pattie had turned up to see him, but, hopefully, he hadn't upset her too much. Where was Angharad though? He had very much hoped, and expected, that she'd be here to see him, now that he was awake and a little more coherent. His sister Carys had left a message on his phone saying that she would visit him during the evening. She said that, although she had not seen Angharad, she assumed that she'd be in to see him during the afternoon. When it became evident that Angharad was not about to appear, Glyn tried to phone her, but without success. He feared that Angharad had once again switched off her phone, although he had no idea why. He sent a text to Carys, asking her to retrieve his telephone charger from his kitchen before she came to visit. *Perhaps Angharad will come this evening.*

Sadly, Angharad did not visit and Carys said that she had not seen her since they were at the hospital previously. She said that she had no idea what the issue was and Glyn asked her not to concern herself. "Angharad will turn up if and when she chooses." Making light of the situation was difficult, and Glyn was feeling increasingly despondent. He tried to recall what had happened when they were last together. *Did I say or do something to upset her? I can't recall anything.*

When Angharad switched on her phone, she noticed a missed call from Glyn. She tried to phone him back, but got no response. She was now scared that Glyn had given up on her – as she had not visited, and she had not answered his call. She went across the yard hoping that Carys was at home. She thanked Carys for sending Pattie to see her, but pointed out that she was now at a loss about what to do next, as Glyn was not answering his phone. Carys told her not to give up on Glyn. She said something similar had happened between her and Jason when a love rival claimed to be carrying Jason's baby – even though, as it turned out, she and Jason had never even had sex together.

"Always give your man the benefit of the doubt in the first instance."

Angharad thanked Carys for her advice and left, saying that she'd give Glyn another call in a while. In truth, she was still concerned. However, as she walked back to her hut, Angharad recalled seeing a notice on the entrance to the ward that Glyn had been moved to. It said that, along with many other wards in the hospital, it offered flexible visiting hours. She hadn't given it much thought after she'd encountered Pattie there. Within 10 minutes, Angharad was driving towards the hospital.

As Angharad approached the bed, she could see that Glyn was dozing. He had a newspaper spread out on top of the bed, but his eyes were closed. Angharad tapped the newspaper gently. "Hi Glyn." Glyn's eyes opened and lit up. He grinned up at her.

"Angharad. You made it." He reached for the bed tilt control and raised it so that he was sitting almost upright. Angharad bent down and kissed him gently, while placing a hand on his cheek.

"Oh Glyn. I'm so sorry about everything that's happened. I owe you a huge apology."

"There's no need to apologise. I had a call from Carys about 10 minutes ago and she told me about what Pattie had said to you. I can understand why you were annoyed with me."

"I was annoyed, yes. But I should have had more faith in you. I was wrong to assume that what Pattie said was true. It didn't make much sense anyway, and I should have spoken to you before condemning you. I hope you can forgive me."

"I'll tell you what – I'll forgive you, if you forgive me for ruining our night out."

Angharad moved a nearby chair, so that she could sit next to Glyn, holding his hand. She smiled. "Consider yourself forgiven. However…" Angharad lifted her hand and wagged her finger at Glyn. "You've been very silly. The surgeon suggested that you've been neglecting your health. Really, Glyn, that burst appendix could have killed you."

"I know, Angharad. I've been a bit sloppy. However, I intend to recover and, hopefully, you'll let me take you on another date."

"I might just allow that. However, you need looking after, and I'm going to be monitoring your health."

Glyn giggled, "I can't think of anyone I'd rather have monitoring my health." Glyn went on to explain that he was likely to be in hospital for a few more days. Apparently, postop recovery from appendicitis was usually fairly rapid. However, the surgeon had told him that the area around his appendix had been severely infected, and he was surprised that Glyn hadn't collapsed much earlier. As a result, recovery would be far slower than normal and Glyn would need to rest for a few weeks before returning to full-time farming work. Even then, he was told to take it easy for a while. Glyn tried to cast a positive light on his misfortune.

"It's not the best time of year for me to be laid up, convalescing, but at least lambing won't start in earnest for a while yet. I may have to contact that pal of yours, Ronny Dennis, if it looks like you and Denny might struggle without me. Still, I have our next date to look forward to, which should help to spur me on."

Chapter 22

Angharad pulled back the curtain and peered out of her hut. She'd been sure that the forecast had been wrong and thought it almost bizarre to have heavy snow in mid-April. It was certainly unusual. Nevertheless, it had been snowing for a while, and it was getting heavier and deeper. It was now beginning to pile up in drifts against the fences and buildings around the farm. She was about to go back to reading her book in the chair next to her multifuel burner when she caught sight of Glyn. He was dragging a couple of bales of hay and lifting them onto an ATV. Immediately, she felt some concern for him. His convalescence had already been delayed by two separate infections – Glyn, predictably, had returned to heavy work far too early, exposing himself to what the doctor described as 'all manner of winter nasties'. Fortunately, Angharad and Denny had coped fairly effectively with lambing, and, with some assistance from Jason, they hadn't needed to approach Ronny Dennis. Lambing was now completed, but Glyn was supposed to be staying indoors, dosing up on antibiotics, and taking it easy, for at least another fortnight.

Although it was Sunday and she was technically 'off duty', Angharad wanted to offer Glyn some help. Since Glyn had returned home from hospital, she'd spent time keeping him company, and helping him with household tasks such as cooking and cleaning, in addition to doing some shopping for him. Angharad would have been happy to spend even more time with him, but as she and Denny were covering much of Glyn's work, her opportunities were limited. Fortunately, Carys had also provided support in the home for Glyn.

By the time Angharad had thrown on a jacket and opened her door, she was just in time to see Glyn going back into the farmhouse, closing the door behind him. She assumed that Glyn intended to take the hay over the hill and down to the ravine where the ewes were inclined to gather for shelter when the weather was bad, especially at times such as this when they would struggle to get at grass anyway. She wondered now, whether Glyn had, perhaps, had second thoughts about venturing out, given his condition and the appalling weather.

About 30 minutes later, Angharad looked out again and the weather seemed to be deteriorating even more rapidly. Indeed, it was difficult to see clearly beyond the boundaries of the yard as the snow now seemed to be blowing almost horizontally. She thought for a moment about knocking on Glyn's door, but decided to take the initiative and drive the ATV over the hill herself. Glyn was not well; he was her boss, and he'd been good to both her and Denny. Nevertheless, it wasn't really for those reasons that she wanted to help him.

♥♥

Having decided that it would be in his best interest to stay warm, rather than venturing out at present, Glyn had gone back into the farmhouse. In addition to the obvious aspects of the weather, visibility was now rather poor and the chill factor in the howling wind was particularly significant. However, as his open fire began to die down, he realised that he would have to leave the house in order to fetch fuel from the barn across the yard. As he looked out, he could see snow drifting against the door so decided to get out there immediately as, if he waited too long, he'd end up having to dig his way into the barn. He was still wearing warm clothing, so simply put on his boots, coat and hat, before leaving the house. However, as he began to cross the yard, he noticed that the ATV which he'd loaded with hay had disappeared. As he approached the spot where it had been parked, the tracks in the snow revealed exactly what had happened. There was a line of faint boot marks leading from the direction of Angharad's hut, along with impressions of the ATV's tyres leading down to the lower yard gate. As the wind eased for a moment, it was possible to see more clearly through the snow and Glyn could just about make out the impression of similar tracks stretching up the Hill towards the turbines. He realised immediately what had taken place and, although he was grateful for Angharad's efforts, he was extremely worried about the possibility that she could get into difficulty. His sense of alarm increased as he recalled that the ATV was almost out of fuel. He swung around and checked the tracks in the yard once more. He could see that Angharad had not driven it to the tank in the yard in order to fill it up before leaving.

Given that the tracks were now quite faint, it seemed that Angharad had been gone for a while. Glyn pulled his mobile phone from his pocket, but there was no signal. He looked up at the hill wondering where she might be. He had no doubt that if, as seemed likely, the ATV had run out of fuel, then Angharad would be in great difficulty and in great danger. Walking back to the farm in such conditions would be virtually impossible. He could only hope that Angharad had sought shelter. However, even if she were to shelter in the depths of the ravine, she'd be subjected to freezing temperatures. He had no option but to go after her. He was, after all, her employer. He was also desperately in love with her.

Angharad knew that she'd made a huge mistake. She'd brought the hay over the hill – as it seemed likely that the ewes would need the extra food if the snow continued to fall. It certainly was continuing, and she was now effectively trapped in the ravine. She had been so stupid – venturing out in weather like this, without even checking the fuel tank on the ATV. She was freezing cold and becoming colder by the minute. She was also petrified. Her feet and her legs felt numb and stiff and her fingers were also tightening up, even though she continually clenched and unclenched her fists. She was wearing warm clothes, vest, shirt, sweatshirt, thick jacket, woolly socks and heavy boots, and yet the cold wind seemed to be drilling through all layers and, like a sneak thief, snatching away much of her body heat. She had moved into the ravine in order to shelter from the worst of the wind. However, she was no longer simply shivering, she was juddering. She was now aware that, if you did become cold enough, your teeth would indeed 'chatter'. She had tried to walk back up the hill, but after a few metres she knew that there was no chance that she'd reach the top, never mind the farm.

There was no signal on her phone and the sky was changing from off-white to grey, as the snow became heavier and the afternoon began to shift towards evening. When she entered the ravine, she could see a sizeable group of sheep, many with lambs, a few metres away deeper inside the cleft. She moved towards them, hoping that maybe she could share some of their warmth, if she could perhaps sit down among them. However, as she approached, they shied away. It was odd that they were skittish in this way, she thought, wondering if they, like her, were uneasy due to the unusual circumstances. Angharad moved back towards the ravine opening and crouched down, curling up into a ball beneath a slate overhang. She felt tears forming as she realised that, if she were still here in the morning, she'd almost certainly be dead. After a while, as the cold continued to tighten its vice-like grip, Angharad's mind began to wander and she experienced flashbacks – glimpses of her past life as a child on the farm that her parents rented, surrounded by chickens and sheep, and, as a young teenager, enjoying music and early boyfriends. Then she saw Neville, flash, sexy Neville. However, life became chaotic as she became pregnant and gave birth to Denny, while, in the background, flash and sexy Neville turned slowly into nasty, hurtful, hateful Neville! Angharad's thoughts leapt forward to her arrival at Tan Y Bryn. She smiled and chuckled, as she remembered her first days at the farm, with Carys, Denny, and Glyn. As she recalled driving to Rhyl on her date with Glyn, a powerful gust of wind dislodged a chunk of snow and ice from the overhang above her, and, as it landed on the side of her head, she was brought cruelly back to the present, and her current awful situation. *What a stupid way for it all to end. I had so much going for me – Denny, my job on the farm, and Glyn. Glyn – I'm so sorry Glyn. After all you've done for me, I've really screwed it all up now. Big time.*

Fortunately, the shed housing the other ATV was in the sheltered corner of the yard, so Glyn was able to open the doors without undue difficulty. He checked the fuel level, climbed on board and turned the key. The machine started immediately, and Glyn mentally congratulated Denny – who normally used it – for keeping it so well maintained. He checked that his jacket was fastened to the neck and, pulling his Indie hat firmly down on his head, he hit the accelerator.

It took quite a while to reach the top of the hill and, by the time he got there, the snow was falling so thickly that visibility dropped to just a few feet. Glyn knew the territory like the back of his hand, so having to use the whirring of the wind turbines to help him orientate himself was strange. Fortunately, the track down to the ravine was easy to follow, as generations of sheep – and sheep farmers – had worn a noticeable groove from the top of the hill to the bottom. While much of the surrounding grass had been kept relatively clear by the high wind, that groove was now filled with snow, making it look like a broad white line running down the middle of a bendy road. Glyn followed it at some speed but eased off the throttle as he sensed the ravine looming. He had no wish to emulate his sister's near disaster when she drove over the edge, and came close to death. For a moment, as he recalled Carys's accident, he felt an additional chill. An omen?

When he spotted the other ATV, his worst fears were realised. There was no sign of Angharad either on or near the machine and he could see from the snow piled up against the tyres and on the seat, that it had been there for a while. It felt a little eerie. Glyn stepped off his ATV and looked around slowly, keen not to miss anything important. He shouted, calling Angharad's name. However, the wind was whistling shrilly through cracks in the nearby rocks and, even in the unlikely event of a response, he'd be unable to hear her, unless she was very close by.

He raised his gloved hand to his face to shield his eyes and, as he looked over towards the opening at the lower end of

the ravine, he could make out a faint trail. Boot tracks.
Angharad!

Glyn located her almost immediately. Angharad was lying curled up on the remains of a hay bale that had been left there a few days previously. The spot at least offered some protection from the wind, although it was quite damp underfoot and the slate overhang looked, and felt, cold.

"Angharad? Angharad? Are you okay?"

Even as he spoke, he realised that his question was an absurd one. He removed his gloves and lifting her head, he was relieved that there was some warmth there. Her eyes opened and, after a few seconds, she smiled up at him – rather weakly.

"Angharad. You have to get out of here. Now!" Glyn's fears for Angharad and for himself were heightened as the wind speed seemed to increase still further, howling, as it blew snow into the overhang. As the group of sheep deep in the ravine watched, Glyn helped Angharad to her feet. He placed his arm around her waist to provide some support but, after taking a few steps up the slope towards the ravine opening, she began to falter, and was obviously about to fall. Glyn dropped into a stoop before her and managed to pull her forward into a 'piggyback 'position. "Put your arms around my neck Angharad. Hold on." As he stood upright, Angharad hung on and Glyn grabbed her lower thighs. Fortunately, Angharad was able to maintain her grip as Glyn staggered out of the ravine and back to his ATV. As Glyn drove back up and over the hill, Angharad sat in the passenger seat, slumped sideways, leaning against him. Although the ATV was fitted with a roll cage and a simple windscreen, it offered only limited shelter from the wind. He could hear her mumbling incoherently, and she began moving her hands around on her lap as if she were trying to hold onto something. Glyn's mind flew back to a short-course he'd attended some years before which compared the impact of hypothermia on new-born lambs with the effect of extreme cold on humans. In addition to the potential for damage to the extremities, feet, hands and face, people suffered temporary confusion and exhaustion along with memory loss and slurred speech. It seemed unlikely that Glyn was going to be able to summon medical help for Angharad, so he needed to get her into the farmhouse and warmed up as quickly as possible.

     As he pulled up outside the house, Glyn climbed from the ATV and opened the door, before returning for Angharad. The short stone pathway was relatively clear as the wind had increased in strength, and was now blowing the snow almost horizontally. Glyn looked briefly at the yard before him, and struggled to see the doors of the lambing shed just a few yards away – such was the ferocity of the blizzard. He lifted Angharad from the ATV and carried her into the house, before laying her on the sofa. Unfortunately, the sofa was a polished leather one with shallow seating, so that if Angharad attempted to roll over, she would probably fall onto the floor. He wondered whether he could perhaps make up a bed for her on the carpet. Glyn decided to get her warmed up before doing anything else – but then remembered that he needed both kindling and logs for the fire, which had now gone out. However, as he peered through the window, he could see deep snow drifting against the shed door, which would take some time to clear using a shovel. He went through to the kitchen to fetch an electric fan heater from the cupboard, and, as it was quite gloomy in the kitchen, he pressed the light switch. Nothing happened. He returned to Angharad, muttering, "Bugger. No fuel, no phone, and now the electricity's gone off."

Angharad, a little warmer now, managed a slurred response. "It never rains but it pours ... or snows, even. Ha!"

"Very funny!" Glyn was relieved that Angharad felt well enough to joke.

Getting Angharad upstairs and into Glyn's bed offered an alternative.

"Angharad. Listen to me. We need to get you upstairs into bed. I can't build up the fire down here at the moment as I have no fuel." Angharad opened her eyes and nodded before struggling into a sitting position.

Glyn helped Angharad to stand and they moved towards the stairs, which were now in near darkness. "Now – how about climbing the wooden hill to Bedfordshire? I don't think I have the strength to carry you up at the moment."

"Will do." He heard Angharad take a deep breath before groping for the bannister rail with her gloved right hand, while placing her left over Glyn's shoulder. She climbed the stairs with only a little support from Glyn – who was delighted by the fact that she seemed to be recovering a little already. He, on the other hand, was beginning to feel distinctly wobbly and, as they reached the landing, it was not clear who was supporting whom. They staggered into the bedroom and Angharad immediately lay down on the bed. Glyn sat down next to her.

"I'm going to let you have a pair of my pyjamas, Angharad. We need to get your boots, socks and trousers off, as everything is damp – which will make it hard for you to get warm. It looks like your jacket and your top are wet too – and you're all covered in mud and sheep poo."

"Okay." Angharad screwed up her face as she gingerly pulled off her gloves, and Glyn reached forward and cupped her hands in his.

"Your hands are like ice. Rub them together for now, and I'll rub them for you in a moment. What about your feet, though?"

"Dunno. Can't feel 'em."

Glyn undid her boots and removed them before pulling off her socks, which were, indeed, very damp. Her toes were cold, so Glyn spent a minute massaging them, hoping there was no permanent damage. With some difficulty, Angharad stood up and unclipped the fastener on the waistband of her trousers. After struggling to push them down over her thighs she asked Glyn to help her and, while he did so, Angharad peeled off her jacket and her sweatshirt. Her vest was visibly damp, too, and she managed to wrench that over her head.

Glyn pulled a tee-shirt and a pair of pyjamas from a drawer unit and placed them on the bed next to Angharad. He also lifted a dressing gown from a hook behind the door.

"You might want to take off your undies – as they look damp. I'm going to use the bathroom." He pulled a heavy blanket from the drawer unit, along with a further tee-shirt and a pair of shorts.

As Glyn moved towards the bathroom door, Angharad spoke. "Glyn. What you did out there was extremely brave – but also very foolish."

Glyn thought for a moment. "If I'd not come after you, where would you have been now? Seriously – you'd have been dead, or pretty close to it. I couldn't let that happen."

"It would have been my own fault, for not checking the fuel in the ATV. Given your condition – you're still convalescing – you could have died too – before you even found me."

"Maybe. But I had to do my best. I had to find you." Glyn opened the door to the ensuite and as he turned to close the door, he caught Angharad's quizzical expression. As he pushed the door to, he added – as if speaking to himself, "I had to. I love you." He assumed, mistakenly, that Angharad had not heard him.

A while later, Glyn came out of the bathroom, carrying his jacket and trousers, both of which were also rather damp.

He had the blanket wrapped loosely around him. Angharad was sitting upright in bed having successfully changed into the pyjamas and dressing gown.

Glyn pointed at her outfit, pleased that she'd managed without support. "Well done. Are you okay?"

"I'm feeling a whole lot better thanks. My fingers and toes are numb and tingly, but least I can feel them. I'll go downstairs and use the sofa."

"What do you mean?"

"Well you don't look very well and I figure that you need the bed more than I do."

"I'm okay, Angharad. You need the warmth. The bed is best for you. I've got blankets that I can put down on the sofa, so I'll be fine." Glyn turned towards the bedroom door, moving perhaps a little too quickly. For a moment, he felt lightheaded, and staggered slightly. Angharad, fearing that he could tumble down the stairs, especially as the remaining light was fading, clambered awkwardly from the bed and called out.

"Glyn. Please! Lie on the bed – if only for a minute. You look really wobbly."

As Glyn lay down, he giggled. "I'm supposed to be helping you – not the other way round. What a sad pair we are."

Angharad pulled the quilt over him and stooped to give him a gentle peck on the cheek. "You speak for yourself Glyn Edwards." She then walked around the bed, lifted the quilt, and cautiously lay on the edge of the bed next to him. She remained, intending to go downstairs as soon as she was sure that Glyn was okay.

Chapter 23

Several hours later, Angharad was awoken by the sound of a cockerel crowing in the pen behind the house. She felt stiff, and was still rather tired – but the ache that she'd experienced in her hands, and especially her feet, had almost gone. Glyn lay with his back to her, snoring softly – and evenly, which Angharad felt was a good sign.

Tiptoeing from the bed, Angharad moved to the window and pulled the curtain back slightly. There was still a little snow in the air but the wind had eased, so the outlook was now more festive than threatening. She could see a security light on across the yard – possibly reacting to snow on the sensor. She turned and could see the time on Glyn's electric bedside clock. The power was back on! Angharad put on Glyn's slippers and crept quietly downstairs to make a drink and slices of toast. As she busied herself in the kitchen, she thought about everything that had led to her current situation. It had been about 15 hours since Glyn found her sheltering in the ravine. He had almost certainly saved her from freezing to death. There was no way that she would have managed to walk back to the farm, and, given the appalling weather, it would only have been a matter of time until she'd have been overcome by the cold. Glyn had been told by his doctor not to exert himself for at least another fortnight and he had, indeed, put himself at great risk in order to search for her. It was evident that he cared about her. Did he, she wondered, simply care about her, or did he care *for* her? And if so, how much?

Angharad placed Glyn's coffee on the bedside cabinet next to him, before climbing back into bed herself. She sat up, leaning back against the headboard sipping her tea. She could see Glyn's form illuminated by the dull early morning light filtering through the curtains. Although he was not particularly handsome in the manner of a typical male heartthrob, he was good-looking in a rugged masculine way. Yes, she thought, he was strong and reliable. He was someone she would be able to depend on, if only he were to make a commitment. Then again, it seemed that he had already made a commitment of sorts on several occasions. Yes – he'd continued to employ her, even after lambing had finished; he saved her from being beaten severely, or worse, by her estranged husband, Neville; after discussion with Jason and Carys, Glyn had arranged for her to live in one of the huts on the farm after Neville had set fire to her house; they'd also been out on a date together – albeit one that had ended disastrously; finally, despite the grave risk to himself, Glyn had ventured out in a snowstorm in order to rescue her and bring her back to the farm. She was fairly sure that she'd also heard him say that he loved her. Of course, he did. Why, then, did she doubt that? Perhaps, her awful experiences with Neville had led her to become rather too cynical, no longer believing that she was in any way attractive or loveable. It seemed that she was sometimes incapable of seeing what was evident, and, even when Glyn paid her compliments, she struggled to acknowledge them. Ultimately, having been married to Neville, she simply had no experience of flattery from men.

    She determined to ask Glyn how he felt about her when he woke up. A few minutes later, she leant over and nudged him gently.

    "Glyn? Are you awake? There's a coffee there for you."

    Glyn coughed gently, before rolling over onto his back. As he did so, he came to rest in such a way that his upper arm was leaning against her thigh. She was momentarily excited to feel the warmth of his body against hers. His eyes opened and he looked up at her. He didn't speak. Rather, he just smiled.

    "I said, there's a coffee there for you." Glyn still remained silent, and continued to smile. Angharad was puzzled, but grinned back at him, before adding, "Glyn – are you okay? You're acting a little oddly."

    "Angharad. I'm fine – but I feel like I died and went to heaven."

    "What are you talking about?"

    Glyn hauled himself upright, and leant next to Angharad against the headboard. He turned and looked directly at her. "I seem to recall you telling me to take a rest after I went a bit wobbly. That was last night. Now, I've just woken up next to you. That's really rather nice. I don't want to make any assumptions, though."

"I know what you mean. I should have slept downstairs on the sofa, but I lay here for a while, just to check that you were okay. But I nodded off too. I guess, after yesterday's fun and games, we were both absolutely knackered." Angharad chuckled.

Glyn took a deep breath. "This situation is downright weird. I mean, I've been fond of you – in love with you, to be honest – for quite some time." Glyn hesitated, as if unsure about whether or not to continue. However, Angharad looked directly into his eyes, smiled, and placed her hand over his. His confidence obviously buoyed, Glyn carried on. "Now, here we are, side-by-side in bed. We didn't finish our first date, and we haven't even kissed, for crying out loud – never mind make love – which is what couples normally do when they find themselves in bed together. As I said, it's weird." Glyn turned his hand so that he could hold Angharad's hand properly. He giggled.

Angharad leant over and kissed him gently on the cheek. As he turned to face her their lips met and they kissed with some passion. Angharad lifted her hand and placed it on his cheek. She said, "I agree. It is a strange way to start a romantic relationship in earnest. We're going to have to make up for lost time. Mmm. I'm thinking that could be fun."

They kissed again and Glyn said, "I'm really enjoying this – but I'm conscious that I haven't brushed my teeth, and I also need a shower. I must stink."

"Mmm! You don't taste too bad – and I know that I need a shower too. Can I share your toothbrush?"

"Of course, you can."

"What about the shower?"

"You want to share the shower? It's not all that big. Do you think we'll both fit inside it?"

Angharad laughed in response. "I wasn't thinking about sharing at the same time – but, then again, now that you mention it ..."

A while later, having consumed toast and coffee, they were sitting in bed, and smiling almost inanely at each other, when the landline phone rang. Glyn lifted the extension from his bedside cabinet. It was Carys.

"Hi Glyn. I'm guessing you've not yet managed to get off the farm. You'll be pleased to know that the snowploughs are out and the main road is passable with some care. Jason and I have made it back as far as the Village Inn where Jaydee and Claudia are handing out free toast and coffees. I've just spoken to Bobby Willis. He's fixed a snowplough blade to his tractor and he's clearing some of the local lanes and driveways. I've persuaded him to clear a path to the farm, and he hopes to start that within the next hour. We'll hang on here until we're confident about getting through."

"Okay Carys. It's great that Jaydee is being so helpful. Being in the Inn has got to be a lot better than sitting in the car, just waiting. How's Willow?"

"Oh, Willow's fine. She slept for much of the way up from Birmingham and she's currently bouncing up and down on Claudia's knee, laughing hysterically. Anyway, how are you Glyn? Are you taking it easy? You know what the doctor said."

"I'm fine thanks Carys. I'm getting loads of rest. In fact, I'm in bed now."

"Good. By the way – have you seen Angharad? I'm a bit concerned about her, alone in that hut. Hopefully she'll stay warm enough. She has some coal and she can also use the electric heater if she needs to."

"I have seen her, and I can confirm that she's quite warm." At that moment, Angharad giggled, loud enough for Carys to hear.

"Where are you Glyn?"

"I'm at home. You phoned the landline, remember?"

"Oh yes, of course. You just told me you're in bed. But who's that I can hear in the background?"

"Oh – it's erm ... the shepherdess. She's here keeping warm, and ... well ... she's helping me to keep warm too."

"Oh right." Carys laughed, and then then spoke loudly – almost shouting – evidently hoping that Angharad would hear her. "Well tell the shepherdess to make sure that you stay tucked in, and that you don't go outside in the snow."

Chapter 24

It was past midday before the lane to the farm was cleared, so that Carys and Jason, were able to return home with Willow. They lit the fire in their half of the house and, while they waited for the place to warm up, they went round next door to join Glyn and Angharad who'd invited them for an early lunch.

As Willow dozed in her carry cot in the corner of the kitchen, Angharad provided the adults with coffee. She asked Jason about the trip home from the midlands. "You finally made it back then? How were the roads from Birmingham?"

Jason shrugged. "To be honest, the drive was fine early on. We started out before six this morning, and, although we didn't see much falling snow, by the time we reached Shrewsbury, there were some patches of snow on the hills. Then, as we drove into Wales, the traffic began to slow as we encountered more and more slush, and eventually snow, on the roads. It said on the news that mid-Wales had been experiencing blizzard conditions since yesterday, but we were optimistic, and we guessed correctly that the gritters and snowploughs would be out in force. As the roads deteriorated, we decided to soldier on, although, given that we had Willow with us, we were a bit uneasy. I have to say that the snow here has obviously been much worse than we realised."

At that point, Carys chimed in. "It is good to be home though. Jason's parents made us very welcome, and they were delighted to see Willow. I have to confess, however, that the city's not for me. There are loads of nice shops, mind – but you can only spend so much time in them, of course."

Jason couldn't resist adding, "And you can only spend so much money in them, of course!"

"Jason!"

As the giggling subsided, Carys's attention turned to Glyn and Angharad's situation. "So – are you two cohabiting now on an ongoing basis – or are you simply keeping each other warm until spring arrives?" Carys laughed, and waggled her index fingers in the air, as she said 'keeping each other warm'. She was gently mocking their earlier exchange on the phone.

Glyn turned to Angharad, winked, and said, "We've not discussed the future in any detail. I'm not sure that Angharad would cope being here with me until spring. We'll talk it through later – and we'll let you know."

Carys nodded. "We'll look forward to that. Erm…" She hesitated, obviously uneasy about something. As Angharad looked at her questioningly, Carys continued. "Tell me to mind my own business if you wish – but I've got to ask this. I mean…it's great to see you two together finally, but…what's been going on here? We both know that you're very fond of each other but, when we left for Birmingham, you were living separately. Now, three days later, you're sharing a bed and, apparently, the house too. I'm just intrigued – about what led to the change, I guess."

Angharad turned to Glyn. "Will you tell them – or shall I?"

♥♥

After Carys and Jason left, Glyn made a couple of phone calls, and he received one from Denny – who was concerned about his mother and whether the farm was accessible. Carys heard Glyn say, "Your mom's fine. She's here. The farm is open now, and it looks as if the thaw is setting in already. However, don't worry about coming in until things have cleared a bit. There's not a lot you can do here at present, anyway. Okay, I'll pass you over to your mom."

Denny was keen to know that his mother was coping effectively, given the snowstorm. Angharad simply told him she was fine and was about to share lunch with Glyn. "I'd be happy to invite you and Lisa over for lunch, too – but, until the roads are clear, I suggest that you stay at home in the warm." As she replaced the receiver, she thought about telling Denny about what had happened during the storm. However, she realised that the story would wait, and she had no wish to worry Denny unnecessarily.

Some time later, when they were alone once more, Glyn said to Angharad. "Do you reckon we'd last until spring?"

"I'd love to spend more time here with you. Perhaps we could try it out and take each day as it comes?"

"Sounds good to me."

The snow melted rapidly over the following few days, and, although it resulted in some fairly heavy flooding in the surrounding areas, life gradually began to return to something close to normal – at least as far as farm activity was concerned. Angharad moved some of her clothes and a few personal possessions from her hut to the house. Her relationship with Glyn was developing slowly, as neither was keen to rush things. Nevertheless, at no point did Angharad regret her move, and she sensed that Glyn was happy with the situation, too.

In fact, it was at about this time that Angharad experienced something of an insight. She was sitting at the kitchen table as Glyn walked in from the hallway. He was smiling at her and said, "Are you okay, love?"

It suddenly struck her that her life had turned a corner. It had been transformed – and she'd only just realised it. Things had been changing for a while, as she and Glyn had grown closer, but there remained a part of her that had struggled to acknowledge her good fortune. Now, after the events of the previous few days, she had absolutely no excuse to feel cursed by her past life. She had no cause to feel unlucky any longer. It seemed almost peculiar that this sensation – an odd mix of relief and joy – should suddenly wash over her in this way, almost like an epiphany. And the reason for the shift in her mood sat down at the table, facing her. Tears started to trickle down her cheeks and she nodded, grinning at him. "I'm just fine,

Glyn. I know that this must sound crazy, but I can't remember the last time I felt like this. It's just so wonderful to feel truly happy. Thank you." Glyn did not say anything in response. He simply nodded, and continued to smile at her. He understood.

As Angharad became more familiar with the house she became increasingly curious about some of its contents.

"Glyn? "I hope you won't think me nosy – but I peeked inside that folder on top of your chest of drawers. I could see some drawings hanging out of it, and was intrigued." Glyn nodded, evidently unconcerned. "There are some lovely images in there. They are not signed though. Do you know who drew them?"

"Oh, those are mine. There's a whole load more in a trunk in the spare room. I've always enjoyed drawing. Nowadays, I don't do quite so much. Carys says that I should try to exhibit them somewhere, or even sell them. I'm not sure though."

"Why not?"

"Well, I tend to draw what I like to see on paper. I don't think I'd enjoy doing stuff just in order to sell it. People probably won't be all that keen on my subject matter."

"Well I reckon the tourists, and some locals, would be delighted to hang some of your work on their walls – especially drawings of recognisable places."

"Do you really think so?"

"Yes – absolutely! It's really good quality. You could frame some to decorate the lounge down at the village inn. Ask Jaydee to sell them for a cut. Alternatively, you could simply attach a small label with your telephone number and a price."

"That's an interesting thought. You really think they're good enough?"

"I'd say they're as good as anything similar that I've seen on sale locally, and better than anything I've ever done."

"So, you draw then?"

"Yes – and I also paint watercolours and use pastels." Angharad hesitated, then frowned. "At least I used to – until my loving husband sold most of my pictures, my paints, my easel, and everything else in order to fund his habit. That was a couple of years back. The few bits and pieces that remained went up in smoke when he set fire to the house. All in all, he was pretty thorough!" Angharad tilted her head and smiled ruefully, before continuing. "I do have a few photos of my efforts on my mobile phone, but that's about it, I'm afraid." Angharad opened up her phone and showed Glyn photos of a small sample of her work, including a watercolour of the river bridge at Llanrwst, and drawings of Conway Castle. Glyn was impressed.

"Wow! You have talent Angharad. I really like the watercolour. You should get back into it. Do you do everything on site – by direct observation as it were?"

"No – not really. I like to do some rough sketches to get a feel for the subject and the environment, but I normally take some photos as well, which I refer to when painting or drawing at home. It's been a while now though."

"That's interesting. I tend to do much the same, myself. I've been thinking about turning the spare room into a sort of art studio. I'm going to buy an easel and a few other bits and bobs. I reckon the light in there could be ideal for drawing and painting. Perhaps you'd like to have a look and let me know what you think."

"I'll certainly have a look and give it some thought. You know, I realised you'd got good taste in art, after you'd bought the fjord prints to decorate the shepherd's hut before I moved into it – but I had no idea you were an artist yourself. How did you first get into it?"

"I used to love drawing as a child. However, my gran and granddad were uneasy about the fact that I'd spend hours at the kitchen table scribbling away – even when the weather outside was fine. Anyway, Gran was rather crafty and asked me to go out to make notes and sketches of what she called problems around the farm – such as damaged fencing, pathways needing repair, and other issues. I remember her saying that I'd be taking on a really important job. Inevitably, perhaps, I swallowed it – hook, line and sinker, and Gran bought me some really nice unlined paper. I didn't spend very much time focusing on fences and paths at that stage, and I soon started to draw sheep, chickens, and eventually, the landscape. The irony was that I'd be out in all weathers – sun, rain, and snow. Kids, eh? What about you?"

"Oh – I got interested in art at school. I was okay at the more academic subjects, especially history and literature – but I've always been more of a hands-on type. They wouldn't let me do woodwork, so I tried my hand at painting and drawing. I dropped it when I met Neville, but, when he started to work away – and, I suspect, play away, too – I bought some watercolours, pastel crayons, and other bits and pieces – and I started doing stuff in my spare time. Art really lowers my stress levels and I've often found that I can become totally absorbed in it. That's been beneficial at times in the past when Neville has played up. He didn't like me to devote time to it though. I think, in his view, it distracted me from focusing on his needs. He expected to be at the centre of my life – always! I got home from work one day, to discover that he'd found a buyer for all of my art equipment, along with the pictures. He'd flogged everything."

"Crikey. I bet you were gutted."

"To be honest, following that, my enthusiasm for an activity that I'd enjoyed for some years had been completely wiped out. I just blanked it out. That's why I've never mentioned it to you before." Angharad was thoughtful for a moment. "I think that was a key turning point in our marriage. Things had been wobbly, almost from the start, but I'd done my best to keep things together, as much for Denny's sake as my own. However, Nev took away my only real outside interest, and used the proceeds for more booze and drugs. It was at that point that I decided that I simply didn't care for him anymore. To be honest, I began to detest him." Angharad paused, turned to Glyn, and smiled. "It's strange. Not so long ago, I'd have found it difficult to even think about all of that, never mind talk about it. It's such a relief to have Neville out of my life. Hopefully, if the divorce goes through okay, and if, as seems likely, he ends up in prison, then he'll be out of my life forever." Angharad took a deep breath and smiled. "There you go, you see. There's probably a little more that you don't know about me, and I'm sure there's loads for me to learn about you. I'm looking forward to finding things out."

"Mmm!" Glyn grinned. "You might find some of it horrifying."

"Somehow, I rather doubt that. By the way…"

"Yes?"

Angharad approached Glyn and placed her hands on his shoulders. "It's been hours since you last kissed me."

Chapter 25

About a month after the blizzard, Angharad moved her remaining clothes and other items from her hut – so that it could be tidied up, ready to be let out to holidaymakers. She was particularly keen to retrieve the small fjord pictures, and she asked Glyn about rehanging them. "How do you feel about hanging them on your living-room wall? I know they could go in the bedroom, but it would be great to have them where visitors could see them."

"I'm fine with that, love – although I'm not sure about hanging them on *my* living-room wall. We're living together, so it's your wall too." Angharad smiled, stepped towards him, looked directly into his eyes for a couple of seconds, and kissed him gently.

"Thanks, Glyn."

The couple moved to the kitchen and Glyn made coffee as Angharad sat at the table compiling a shopping list.

Glyn placed the drinks on the table and sat down next to Angharad, before continuing. "At some point, it would be good to travel to Norway to see the fjords for real. We could do some sketching and take some photos – and, then, perhaps we could have a go at producing our own pictures – you know, painting, drawing, watercolours or whatever."

Angharad was thoughtful for a moment. "Glyn?"

"Yes love."

"I've been thinking about Pattie."

Glyn was momentarily stunned. "Pattie? My ex-girlfriend? Why have you been thinking about her?"

"Well, when she came to see me in my hut – in order to apologise for lying to me – she did tell me a bit about your relationship, and why it ended. She said that you two were incompatible. Your interests were simply different. She described you as a bit of an adventurous outdoorsy sort, while, as far as I could gather, she's into comfy chairs and sitting by the fireside."

"That's probably not far from the truth. We got on well for a good while but, as things started to get more serious between us, it was difficult to see how things would develop in the future. What I mean is – we just didn't seem to want the same things. We could have ended up living with each other, in the same house, but, at the same time, living separate lives – like passing ships in the night, if you get my drift."

"And how do you think our relationship could develop?"

"I'm more optimistic about us – especially as we seem to have quite a few common interests." Glyn paused, looking concerned. "What do you think? You're not worried about us, are you?"

"Worried? No, not at all. I agree with what you say about our common interests, but I think it might be good to talk things through in more detail. It's worth keeping in mind that our situation is hardly typical. I mean, we're fairly mature, and I won't be having any more children – so we won't have that to bind us together. It might be nice to consider the interests that you refer to – in order to see how we can develop them. What do you reckon?"

"That sounds like a good idea to me – although I can't honestly imagine us turning into a couple of television watchers. Having said that, it would be all too easy to retreat to the settee in the living room in the evenings, I suppose."

"The settee's fine sometimes, but not every evening."

"No – some evenings, we might want to play upstairs!" He leaned towards her, slid his hand beneath the table and placed it on her thigh.

"Glyn. Behave yourself!" Angharad turned towards him, grinning. "Later!"

Angharad and Glyn spent the early evening discussing their relationship – and potential future developments. They both felt that living together was a dream come true, but they agreed that, while having a sense of routine helped to limit day-to-day stresses, it was important to retain a sense of adventure – especially as far as their personal and shared experiences were concerned. Angharad retrieved an unused notepad and a biro from a kitchen drawer. "Let's jot down a few ideas for starters. Then we can think about how we can move things forward."

As Angharad lifted the pen, Glyn pointed to the pad. "Heading: Art." Over the next hour, they generated notes about developing their studio, visiting galleries and exhibitions, undertaking field trips, locally and further afield to look for potential subjects for drawing and painting. Glyn said that, given that they both enjoyed photography – for its own sake, as well as for generating quick studies to inform drawing and painting – they might benefit from a couple of new cameras.

Angharad said that she would like to develop the garden at the rear of the house, as well, and she suggested that, eventually, it might be worth moving the chicken hutch out of the garden, or maybe even investing in a bigger one – perhaps to produce and sell eggs. "Do you think it might be worth keeping chickens that lay blue eggs? I remember we had some when I was a child, and they used to sell well at market. Legbars, I think the hens were called." She paused for a moment. "I'm sorry Glyn. My mind is all over the place. I've shifted into business mode now. Chicken rearing and blue eggs are hardly shared leisure activities. Seriously – there's so much on the horizon that is fresh and novel. There's so much to look forward to: there's art, there's watching Willow grow, and even work about the farm is potentially exciting, especially with the farm shop and the holiday lets."

Glyn laughed. "Don't apologise, Angharad. Your enthusiasm is infectious. As well as seeing Willow develop, it'll be interesting to see how well Denny progresses on his college courses, particularly given the skills that he demonstrates about the farm. I'll speak to Carys about changing his job title from 'junior trainee' to just Assistant Farm Manager. We could simply call him Farm Manager, but I need a job, too."

Angharad laughed, and said, "Denny will love that. Thanks Glyn."

"I think there's a lot more to talk through – but we could do with more notepads. I have a pack of them upstairs somewhere."

He found a pack of six pads in a box in the spare room and, as he walked back out onto the landing, Angharad was climbing the stairs towards him, smiling. "I was thinking, Glyn. Maybe we should continue our discussion in bed!"

"Angharad – you're really rather naughty."

When they eventually returned downstairs, Angharad and Glyn took two notepads each. They used one for jotting down potential leisure projects and activities, and the other for work-related notions. They decided to compare notes every week, before entering significant leisure issues into a 'joint' notepad. They'd then use the notepad as a sort of primer for planning both short and long-term activities. Glyn was keen to do something similar with the work notepads, and Angharad suggested a development.

"What if the farm-related ideas were transferred into an online document which could then be accessed by Carys, Jason, and Denny. It could be included as a discussion point on the business meeting agenda – or it might even form the basis of the agenda itself, after others have had the chance to 'chip in'."

"Now that is a brilliant idea. You're not just a pretty face, Angharad."

"You say the nicest things, Glyn." She turned towards him, raising one eyebrow. "I think!"

Chapter 26

Following Neville's agreement to the divorce, Angharad had contacted a solicitor who filed the necessary paperwork for her. The process was straightforward and, by the end of April – shortly after the blizzard – Angharad received a letter informing her that Neville had responded positively. It appeared that, despite being incarcerated. Neville was handling all correspondence promptly, possibly because he had also received a date for an initial court hearing. He faced charges for theft, burglary and grievous bodily harm. In May, Neville's case came to court. Despite Angharad's fears to the contrary, the initial hearing was something of a non-event, as Neville pleaded guilty to all charges, and was referred to the Crown Court for sentencing. It was a further three months before Neville was sentenced and at no time had any of his victims – Angharad, Denny, Glyn, or Kelly Garcia – been required to attend court. Neville was sentenced to 12 years in prison, with a recommendation that he serve at least eight years behind bars. Angharad's divorce from Neville had been finalised just a couple weeks before he was sentenced. Angharad finally began to experience a sense of closure.

Chapter 27

Two years later:

Angharad had driven from the farm early, in order to shop at the supermarket in Bangor. She enjoyed shopping on her own, almost as much as she loved shopping with Glyn or Carys. Also, it was good to escape sometimes, as life at Tan Y Bryn could be quite hectic, even though she and Glyn were able to take time out together which they devoted to joint interests and occasional trips away. The business had expanded and, in addition to farming sheep, there was a farm shop and café, holiday lets, and even a free-range egg side-line. Although Angharad was involved in all aspects of the business, she had overall responsibility for the farm shop and café, and the free-range hen houses and paddocks. The shop and café were now open all year round, picking up considerable passing trade, especially during the summer months. They were selling their own produce and a couple of nearby farms were also selling stuff through the shop. Locally sourced produce included ewes' milk and cheese, along with fruit and vegetables. The egg business was developing well, and was selling to several shops in the area, along with pubs and restaurants, both locally and in the north Wales resorts. The holiday lets were beginning to make some money, especially since Denny had taken responsibility for marketing. Yes – things were, indeed, hectic, though nevertheless, enjoyable.

Angharad strolled casually along the bakery aisle looking for wholemeal scones – Glyn's favourites. Her concentration was drifting as she considered how profoundly her circumstances had changed and how pleasurable her life was as a result. She reached out and grasped one end of a pack of scones, just as another hand gripped the other end. She turned, apologising as she did so.

"Oh, sorry." The woman facing her looked familiar. "Lucy? It is you, isn't it?" Her ex-neighbour, the woman who'd lived in the house next door to the one that Neville had burned down, took a moment to recognise her.

"Angharad? Gosh how lovely to see you."

After exchanging pleasantries, Angharad and Lucy arranged to meet in a nearby café, after finishing their shopping.

It was wonderful to talk about old times over coffee. Angharad told Lucy a little about her life on the farm – and how she'd been living with Glyn for almost two years. "My life has changed enormously, and very much for the better. I've been busy helping to develop the business, and Denny has been heavily involved, too."

Lucy said that Angharad's old house had been rebuilt – although it took the landlord a long time to get it sorted. Apparently, Lucy's new neighbours were pleasant – but quite elderly, and not nearly so lively as the house's 'previous occupants'.

Angharad joked, "You mean you miss the shouting and screaming when Neville was about?"

"I didn't really mean that – although your relationship was a bit sparky at times. I did read about his trial, and I admit that I wasn't surprised when he went to prison. What he did to that American woman, and what he did to you and Denny was simply horrible."

"Well, to be honest, his punishment was no more than he deserved, although I know that some people thought he actually got off lightly with a twelve-year sentence."

"You're not still married to him, are you?"

"No way. I'm happy to say that he didn't contest my divorce petition. I just hope that I never see him again – even though he hardly presents a threat to anyone anymore."

"What do you mean?"

"Oh, didn't you hear? It was about six months ago. As I understand it, Neville had been annoying some of the other prisoners – he never did know when to keep his mouth shut. Anyway, the story goes that he tripped and fell down some stairs – although it was suggested that someone helped him on his way. He damaged his upper spine and is now almost totally paralysed. He only gets about using an electric wheelchair. He was moved from the prison to a hostel in South Wales. Rough justice, I suppose."

"Golly. How do you feel about that?"

Angharad thought for a moment. "Perhaps I should feel bad about it, given that I was married to him for nearly twenty years. Also, he's Denny's father but, to be honest, I feel indifferent. I simply don't care. I know Denny feels the same way."

"That makes sense, I suppose. There's nothing you can do to change the situation now, and, given how things have moved forward for you, and for Denny, there's no point looking back. You seem to have a much better life now, with a lot more to look forward to."

"Oh yes." Angharad smiled. "Yes, indeed!" She hesitated once more – thoughtful. "It's odd. A while back, I was thinking about how much happier I am now, than in the past. It occurred to me that at least a small part of the reason for that is that I'm no longer afraid."

"Afraid?"

"Yes. When I was with Neville, I was constantly on edge – even when he was away from home. I never knew what sort of mood he'd be in when he returned. I lived in a sort of constant state of anxiety. With Glyn, it's so different. We do have occasional disagreements, but, even if I really manage to annoy him – the worst he'll do is put his hands on his hips, and frown at me. I'm likely to end up in fits of laughter. With Neville though, I'd get a black eye, or worse."

After saying goodbye to Lucy, Angharad made her way back to her car. Seeing her old neighbour had bought back memories, some good, some bad. She recalled a handful of significant events that took place when she was living at her old home: it was where she had raised Denny and many years later, while living there, she started working as a shepherdess at Tan Y Bryn, where she met Glyn. Then, of course, Neville had returned, burned the house down, and created wicked mayhem for her and Denny, and for Glyn. Ultimately though, things certainly seemed to have worked out for the best and she was now happier than at any time in her adult life.

Most evenings along with occasional weekends were spent with Glyn, engaged in their shared hobbies of photography and art. At that time, Angharad was working on some paintings of Norwegian fjords, an activity she described as a vanity project: she was doing the paintings for her and Glyn's pleasure, as they'd recently returned from a 10-day fjords cruise. Glyn and Angharad's interest in art had become a major factor in their lives, to the extent that they had turned one of the rooms in the house into a studio. They were both selling pictures through the farm shop and café, and over the internet, and some of Angharad's work had even begun to attract the attention of dealers further afield. The same company that had helped the farm set up internet facilities had also helped them to construct a site advertising their artwork. Things were selling surprisingly well – and Lisa, who worked as an administrator at a marketing company, suggested that they might try producing and selling greetings cards featuring images of local places and landscapes. She said that such 'local' art might prove popular and could well sell at a premium price.

Chapter 28

Glyn and Angharad had invited Carys and Jason round to their house for a coffee. However, beforehand, as Glyn entertained his two-year-old niece, Willow, downstairs, Angharad showed their visitors a range of images in their remodelled studio. Both Carys and Jason were impressed – with the studio, and with its contents. In addition to a couple of easels, there were cupboards and racks containing art materials, along with a computer with an additional monitor and a large format printer. There were also hundreds of photos and dozens of drawings and paintings of various types and sizes – many of which were of recognisable places, local and distant, along with a handful of still life and portraits of friends and relatives. When they returned downstairs, Angharad presented them with a framed painting of their daughter. "I based this on one of photos I took of her a couple of weeks back. I know it will soon look out of date – as she's growing so quickly. Still, I'll enjoy painting another."

    Jason said, "Angharad – both you and Glyn are stunningly talented, and you seem to be growing more skilful by the day. I don't know how you find the time, given that you both work so hard around the farm."

    Glyn, quick off the mark, responded. "Well, Jason, it's like this. I do most of the work, but Angharad is simply brilliant at making herself *look* busy. She pops in and out of the house at strategic moments – usually when other people, such as you, Carys, and others happen to be passing. You'll notice, too, how she seems to exude a sense of energy, as she scurries about at high speed."

Jason nodded. "So, what you're saying, Glyn, is that she's simply more creative than you are?"

As Angharad leant down and retrieved a poker from the rack next to the log burner, Glyn said, "Yes, that's it. She's very, very creative." He turned towards the kitchen. "I'll do us all a coffee."

Angharad, waving the poker, said, "Ha! Now who's being creative, Glyn Edwards?" Even after living together for almost two years, humour was still a key feature of Glyn and Angharad's relationship.

In addition to sharing the occasional coffee, Glyn and Angharad and Carys and Jason had been routinely meeting up for an evening meal at least once a month, usually on Friday. Occasionally, they would go out to a restaurant in a nearby town, while Denny and his girlfriend Lisa babysat Willow. At other times, they would eat at home – either at Glyn's or at Carys's. They had also begun inviting Denny and Lisa at such times – not to babysit – but, rather to share the occasion.

One Friday, at Carys and Jason's, after the meal, the group moved through to the lounge, where they sat down with coffee. The meal had been prepared by Carys and Angharad and Glyn complemented them.

"That meal really was a bit special. I'm wondering whether we should turn the farm shop and café into some sort of boutique restaurant. We could install you two as the chefs – given that your culinary skills are so impressive."

"Carys was quick to respond. That's a good idea. We'd have to charge premium rates for Friday evening family get-togethers, though – and I'm not sure that you'd be able to afford us, Glyn." Angharad, laughed, nodding in agreement.

Conversation continued for a while, until Denny spoke up. "Excuse me folks. Lisa and I have something we'd like you all to hear. You're all aware that Lisa and I have been exploring the possibility of renting our own house. Living at Lisa's has been good, and Lisa's parents have been wonderful. However, the house is not particularly large, and things can feel a bit cramped at times. Also, as we look to the future, we'd like the freedom to make our own decisions and do more of our own thing. On top of that, we feel that setting up home together signals a firm commitment to each other." Denny hesitated, before continuing. "Anyway, we looked at a few rental properties, and we've taken on a small semi-detached cottage. It's not that far from here, on the other side of the village – just past the primary school. We'll pick the keys up tomorrow, and, we'll start moving in over the weekend. We hope to have the place fit for occupation by the end of the week. Oh…and Lisa has something to say."

Lisa looked around, a little nervously. "Our aim is to have a house warming next Saturday, and you're all invited. My mom and dad will be there too, along with a couple of our friends. My cooking skills are nothing like those we've enjoyed tonight – but I'm going to give it my best shot. I do hope you can all come." Lisa smiled, more confident now, as those around her smiled back and nodded in acceptance. As the evening progressed, conversation focused on a range of topics, but especially on Denny and Lisa's move. By the time the couple left for home, Jason and Glyn had offered to help them with their house move, and Carys and Angharad had offered to help with the catering for the house warming.

♥♥

The house-warming party was a success. Lisa's parents had been to the farm before, and had also been to a Christmas get-together at the village inn. As a result, they knew Glyn and Angharad well, and they'd also met Carys and Jason. The atmosphere at Lisa and Denny's house was relaxed and jovial. Part way through the evening, Denny signalled that he had an announcement to make.

"Firstly, Lisa and I would like to thank you all for coming. We'd like to thank you for the gifts you've bought for us, and we'd like to thank those of you who have helped with the move – especially Jason and Glyn." Turning to Lisa, he added, "and I know Lisa wants to thank my mom and Carys for helping with the food, which was…well…'yummy'." It was evident from the cheer that went up, that everyone present had been impressed with the mixed buffet. "We'd both like to propose a toast to Lisa's parents, Ellie and Ron, for their support and for putting up with me for so long."

The room erupted with laughter, when Glyn chipped in with, "No easy feat, I imagine!"

"Thanks for that Glyn. And in spite of that, I must thank Glyn – and Carys – for all that they've done for me since I began working at the farm. They've been really great to work for." Denny stepped to one side and picked up a carrier bag, from which he withdrew a framed certificate. "I almost forgot. My Diploma in Farming Business Management arrived a couple of days ago, and I had it framed."

"Glyn called out, well done Denny. You deserve it." and he led the applause.

Jason then added, "There you go, Denny. He does have your interests at heart." Denny and Glyn both grinned in response to a shared joke from the past.

As the noise subsided, Denny lifted his hands, indicating that he had more to say. "Finally – I'd like to thank my partner Lisa for being such a lovely – and loving – girl. We have talked about getting engaged, but we feel we're a bit young to start thinking about marriage. Maybe next year. However, in the meantime, I bought her an eternity ring, which I'm praying she'll accept now." Denny pulled a ring case from his pocket and opened it. He held it, so that Lisa could remove the sapphire and diamond eternity. She slipped it onto her finger, before throwing her arms around Denny.

Glyn called out, "Nice one, Denny." He held up his glass, and looking around at others in the room, he added, "Good luck to the pair of you." Everyone else raised their glasses, echoing Glyn's words.

Angharad had moved to Glyn's side and, as she grabbed his free hand, she whispered in his ear. "And nice one, Glyn." He turned to face her and winked.

A little later, at their own home, Glyn and Angharad reflected on the evening. Angharad said, "I think Denny and Lisa are wise to hold off on marriage for a while. Even if they are absolutely sure about each other, a wedding can be quite an expensive affair these days – and they're still very young, so there's no rush anyway.

Glyn nodded. "I'd expect nothing less from Denny. For a youngster, he is very mature – and almost a bright as his mom!"

"Compliments, eh? What are you after Mr Edwards?"

"Nothing. He is a good lad, though, and Lisa's a lovely girl. I can just see them getting married. Who knows – you could be a granny before too long."

"Hmm! Granny Angharad, eh? I'm not so sure about that."

"You'd love it. Look how you are with Willow." Glyn's reference to Carys and Jason's daughter brought a wide smile to Angharad's face. She enjoyed spending time with the toddler, who called her Angad.

Chapter 29

The morning after the event, Glyn and Angharad were at home, rearranging their studio. Glyn had been moving a few sketches into a storage box, in order make space on a table. He sat down on a stool and watched as Angharad similarly tidied her materials on the other side of the room. After a minute or so, Angharad became aware that Glyn was watching her.

"Are you okay Glyn? You're very quiet."

"Oh, I'm just admiring the view."

Angharad looked towards the window, puzzled, as she could tell that Glyn was not looking in that direction, but at her. "It is a lovely view – but it's out there, not over here!"

"You're right. It is a lovely view, but the lovely view that I'm admiring is over there." Glyn pointed at Angharad, who turned to face him. She placed her hands on her hips and tilted her head slightly, narrowing her eyes, but failing to conceal a smile.

"What are you talking about? Out with it. I can see something's bothering you."

Glyn giggled. "Did I ever tell you that you've got a lovely bum for an oldie?"

"Have I?" Angharad looked down at her lower body. "I don't know about 'lovely' – but I'm certainly not carrying too much excess fat. I work too hard to accumulate any."

"Oh – so I'm working you too hard now, am I?"

Angharad laughed. "No. Not at all. But I've always enjoyed working hard around here. I'm just trying to impress the boss, I guess."

Glyn shifted back on his chair and pointed to his own lap. "Sit!"

"Sit?" Angharad did her best to look indignant as she stepped across the room and sat down on Glyn's lap, throwing her arms around him and kissing him firmly on the lips. "Sit? I'm not a blooming dog, you know."

"No, you're not – which is just as well, as I'd expect you to round up the sheep."

Angharad started to protest, but Glyn placed a finger on her lips. "Seriously, Angharad. We've been together for a while now, and I for one have enjoyed almost every minute of it. I love you. Big time!"

"Well – I love you too, even when you treat me like Mollie the collie." They both laughed, and Angharad continued. "You gave me a second chance at life – quite literally, when you carried me back in the snowstorm. And you also gave me a second chance at living." She looked from the window at the early summer meadows and the wooded hills beyond – a glorious vista – and her gaze panned around the room, at the photos, sketches, drawings and paintings that bore testimony to many shared hours devoted to their common interests. "You were – and still are – my knight in shining armour, if you get my drift."

"I do indeed. It was the very least I could do." Glyn hesitated, remembering an exchange from the distant past. "Your knight in shining armour, eh? Sir Glyn of Tan Y Bryn?"

"Sir Glyn of Tan Y Bryn? Crikey – where did that come from?"

For a moment, Glyn's thoughts leapt back to his gran, and to a lonely looking mug on the drainer downstairs "I'll tell you about it later." Angharad sat quietly for a moment, gazing into Glyn's eyes. She knew him well enough to sense that he had more to say. "Do you remember that conversation we had when we found ourselves in bed together, following the snowstorm? We'd come a long way together, without really engaging with each other physically."

Angharad interrupted. "Yes – I remember. It felt as if we'd been walking side-by-side, but without holding hands. I said we'd need to begin the journey again, and that we were going to have to make up for lost time."

Glyn nodded. He hesitated, and then said, "Do you think we've made up for that lost time yet?"

"I'm not sure – but I think we've made good use of the time we have spent together. I've certainly enjoyed it – and I'm still loving it. Why do you ask?"

"Well … I was wondering if we should get married. There's no pressure, mind. I guess I'm aware that Denny and

Lisa could be stealing a lead on us. It's not a problem, though … I mean … if you'd prefer not …" Angharad placed her finger on Glyn's lips, silencing him.

"I thought you'd never ask." Angharad smiled, and Glyn grinned in response. Angharad added, "I'm not entirely sure about the nature of the proposal, though."

Glyn, lifted Angharad from his lap, and then stood up himself. He smiled and pointed to the seat of the chair. "Sit!"

Angharad did as instructed. "I'm back to being Mollie the collie, am I?"

"Maybe. But I'd much rather you were Mrs Angharad Edwards." Glyn knelt on the floor before Angharad and took her hand …

Glossary of terms

(including those specific to the North Wales setting)

Anglesey: an island off the coast of North Wales.
Bangor: a university town in North Wales.
Betws: this refers to the small town of Betws-y-Coed (The Prayer House in the Wood), in North Wales.
bloke: man.
bob: shilling. An informal reference to pre-decimal UK currency.
bollocks: (vulgar) testicles.
bonkers: insane (often used affectionately).
border collie: a popular farm dog, most often used for herding sheep.
blighter: a person (often someone who is envied or unliked).
blimey: an exclamation of surprise.
bugger: a mild expletive (synonym for sodomise).
buzzard: European common buzzard (NOT a vulture. Similar to an American hawk).
crackers: daft, slightly crazy.
ensuite: a bathroom attached to a bedroom.
frig: have sexual intercourse.
handle: name.
lard-arse: (vulgar) obese person.
Llanrwst: a small town in North Wales.
mind: sometimes used instead of 'mind you', or 'be aware'.

mobile home park: trailer park.

mobile phone: cell phone.

old banger: old car or van.

pear-shaped: awry, wobbly, incorrect.

settee: sofa

slapper: a promiscuous woman or prostitute.

Snowdonia: the area and mountain range in North Wales.

Tan y Bryn: In Welsh, this means 'Below the hill'.

tupping: mating female sheep (ewes) with the ram (tup).

Summary of Book 1

The Ravine – The first tale from Yan Y Bryn
(Just in case you missed it …)

Shepherdess and farm co-owner, Carys Edwards, is bright, resourceful, and attractive. Oh – and she's lonely! It seems that few eligible men are keen to engage with a 33-year-old woman who spends much of her time wrestling with sheep, working outdoors from dawn until dusk, and in all weathers.

Her boyfriend, Gavin, is married – but assures her that he'll soon be free of his wife. Carys has her doubts, and, while on a college course, she meets another man who shows an interest in her.

While this is happening, Jason, a self-employed solicitor and contact writer takes up residence in the modernised shepherd's hut which is available to let on the mid-Wales farm. He's good looking, sociable – and, to say the least, intriguing. Sadly, though, he shows little interest in Carys.

Her late grandmother had joked that Carys could end up on the shelf. An old maid in fact … Some joke!

In the circumstances, Carys could perhaps be forgiven for wondering if life could become any more challenging …

This is a tale of romance in the hills of Southern Snowdonia. It features characters from radically different backgrounds and it tells of the hazards arising when we make casual assumptions about those around us.

Sometimes, things – and people – are not at all what they seem, and misunderstandings can be costly!

Printed in Poland
by Amazon Fulfillment
Poland Sp. z o.o., Wrocław